The Most Cunning Heart

ALSO BY CATHERINE GRAHAM

POETRY

Æther: An Out-of-Body Lyric

The Celery Forest

Her Red Hair Rises with the Wings of Insects

Winterkill

The Red Element

Pupa

The Watch

FICTION

Quarry

The Most Cunning Heart

Catherine Graham

Palimpsest Press
1171 Eastlawn Ave.
Windsor, Ontario, N8S 3J1
www.palimpsestpress.ca

Printed and bound in Canada
Cover design and book typography by Ellie Hastings
Edited by Ginger Pharand
Copyedited by Theo Hummer

Palimpsest Press would like to thank the Canada Council for the Arts and
the Ontario Arts Council for their support of our publishing program. We
also acknowledge the assistance of the Government of Ontario through the
Ontario Book Publishing Tax Credit.

This is a work of fiction. Any resemblance to actual events or persons living or
dead is coincidental. The opinions expressed are those of the characters and
should not be confused with the author's.

LIBRARY AND ARCHIVES CANADA CATALOGUING IN PUBLICATION

TITLE: The most cunning heart / Catherine Graham.
NAMES: Graham, Catherine, author.
IDENTIFIERS: Canadiana (print) 20220142564
             Canadiana (ebook) 20220142580

ISBN 9781990293122 (SOFTCOVER)
ISBN 9781990293139 (EPUB)
ISBN 9781990293146 (PDF)

CLASSIFICATION: LCC PS8563.R31452 M67 2022 | DDC C813/.6—DC23 *for John Coates*

The most cunning heart—it's beyond help.
Who can figure it out?

—Jeremiah 17:9 *Common English Bible*

I

Last night the wind howled with slashes of rain against my loft window, the skylight. On and off like a light switch. I thought of the other sounds I'd encountered since my arrival in Northern Ireland, the wide range of accents. Declan's lyrical lilt, a stark contrast to his Goth demeanor. Iris, the mature student with a chip on her shoulder—she was from East Belfast, always eyeing me. And the two twenty-something Americans, Beth and Helen, who were younger than I was by a few years that felt like decades. Loss. It catapulted you into an unwanted maturity.

The quarry had been an easy sale. How could it not be, with its blue oval beauty? Surrounded by a ring of deciduous and evergreen trees, the water-filled blasted limestone was coated with spines from lost lives.

Living next to the Irish Sea made me long for the quarry again—the water, the sunfish, our bungalow, Mom and Dad watching me dive off the dock.

Showered and dressed, I climbed down the loft ladder. Last night's fire had pearled to ash—turf, harvested from bogs—but the peat scent lingered. *Fractal crackles*. I'd worked hard on my poem for today's workshop. Now I was afraid to look at it.

Mom loved watching a fire. Those winter months her athletic body was leaving her, she sat in the living room, her mind alive like the quick licks of light. When I asked, "What is it, Mom? What are you thinking?" she smiled and said, "Nothing, Honey."

I opened the mini-fridge in the galley kitchen and pulled out the jar of red jam. It was thoughtful of Mrs. Petty to have stocked the cottage with essentials before my arrival. The milk, bread, and cheese had long been consumed, but the jam lasted. Mrs. Petty had greeted me in the driveway after Janet and Benny picked me up from the airport that bleary-eyed morning. She must've been peering out the farmhouse window when she saw their mud-red car zig-zagging down Portmuck Hill towards the farmhouse; my cottage with the red door was tucked in the back.

With my cup of tea and plate of toast I sat by the fireplace and looked at my poem in the three-ring notebook. The first line wasn't bad—

A knock at the window made me jump. Mrs. Petty peered in. I opened the cottage door.

"Ten o'clock on the dot, I'll be leaving for Larne tomorrow. Meet me out front."

"Oh, I have classes then."

"Oh, no you don't, Caitlin. I already talked to Benny. They've been cancelled. Ta," she said and walked away in her Wellingtons.

I suppressed the urge to slam the door. What if I'd been half-naked? Friendly? Nosy more like it. Was I being too harsh? There was no phone in the cottage. But peeking in? She would've seen my bras and panties strewn on backs of chairs, now dry and stiff from last night's fire. I was too shy to hang them on her clothesline.

But if I closed the front curtain, I wouldn't see out.

When the mist and rain weren't pressing in, the Ulster sky was enormous. Blue dazzled with a vibrancy I couldn't recall from home. As if the skin of the sky had been birthed again and again, blue-clean from all that rain. Birds darted in and out of trees and hedgerows. With my knapsack strapped on my back and my poem inside it, I breathed it all in.

While walking up the hill to the House of Poets, an elegant black and white bird, smaller than a robin, landed in front of me. It scurried in bursts before stopping to wag its long narrow tail. What did that mean? Could I use it in a poem? This newness was exciting but overwhelming at times. Simple things were a challenge. How was I to know a plastic switch had to be flicked on to make the electricity work to heat the kettle? And that white string dangling from the ceiling in the tiny upstairs shower had to be pulled for hot water. I goosebumped my way through that first one, so cold cold cold.

Mrs. Petty and Janet thought it was cute, my helplessness. *Caitlin Maharg, the silly Canadian.* Being quiet didn't help either. I was like Mom that way. I closed my eyes to hear her voice. The sound of the sea.

I wasn't comfortable walking into the House of Poets without knocking first, but Benny and Janet insisted we five M.A. students do that. "It's your house too," they said.

"Hello?" No answer.

A house *and* a school. I didn't tell Aunt Doris that; she'd be curious and rightly so. "It sounds like a cult. Is it a cult? How long has this program been running? The first year? Who are these people? What are their credentials? You're paying *that* much to go there? What about your teaching job?" Taking this journey was so unlike me. But losing both parents, along with the quarry—my family home—had changed everything.

I thought of the woman who'd drowned herself in the quarry, the need to escape, to put an end to what can't be lived through. Stone, ankle, rope.

I was in New Hampshire at the Robert Frost Place when I first heard about the program from a Dublin poet. Sharing poems with strangers had proved to be hard psychic work. Somehow it helped to remember Mom's phrase: *Keep your eye on the ball.* But I couldn't always do that.

Niamh sat alone in the corner during the nightly house parties, sipping her dram of whiskey, her bony frame in a hunch. That last night I pulled up a chair and sat down beside her. What made me do this, I still don't know.

In no time at all we opened up in ways that never seem to happen with those you've known for years. Friends think they know you, but they don't.

"Yes, poetry helps," she said and took another sip. "It's helping me, I tell you. My goddamn husband doesn't want me but wants to keep me trapped. No divorce in Ireland. And it's the 19-goddamn-90s. You married?"

I shook my head. Marrying never appealed to me, but the thought of my father walking me down the aisle did. I would never have that.

"Spend time on poetry then. Master the craft. You enter history when you attempt it. It's daunting and overwhelming, but keep pushing through. Ever think of doing an M.A.?"

"In poetry? There's nothing like that in Canada." Did she mean the United States?

She pulled a notebook from her purse. "Here, write down your address. There's a new school outside Belfast. I'll send you details."

"Caitlin," said Janet, coming down the stairs. She was dressed in her usual: black tunic and tights, black mules. To hide her plumpness? I never understood that fashion trick. Black absorbed light like grief. It made you notice what cancelled colour.

"Didn't Mrs. Petty tell you?" she said. "No classes today."

"Isn't Andy Evans coming—"

"He can't make it. He's terribly sick. A cold that's gone bad, I think—"

"But my poem—"

"Think of today as a writing day. We all need those." Squeezing by me, she headed into the tiny kitchen. I followed, my mind still taking in the news to rearrange my emotions, the pre-nerves that came before workshopping still roaming inside me.

And now a twist of anger. That's twice a visiting poet has cancelled. Janet flicked on the red switch and turned on the kettle. "Benny needs his morning tea. He's working on a poem upstairs." She giggled. "He likes to work in bed." She shoved two sauce-stained plates into the dish-stacked sink, ignoring the clattering. I flinched. *What's that smell? Rotting cheese?*

"And no classes tomorrow," I said.

"Mrs. Petty's taking you to Larne, isn't she? You'll get an eye opening there."

I was quiet on the drive to Larne. The morning rain had ceased but the sky was low and misty. Little rain-beads clung to the stillness of things like oval birds hanging upside-down on wires and branches. They jewelled the hedgerows with sunlight that wasn't there.

Mrs. Petty was slick with her stick shift. She used it like an extension of her wiry body. She lived alone in the farmhouse that faced land, not water, despite the stunning sea view. On a clear day you could see Scotland, the Mull of Kintyre. My mother's side came from the Isle of Mull. They left everything they knew to farm the craggy fields near Owen Sound.

The sea held liquid beauty, but land was the prized possession. Water was for traffic. It couldn't be claimed, parcelled out, divided. I'd witnessed the soldiers roaming the streets of Belfast my one visit there since my arrival. Dressed in army fatigues and carrying rifles. Manning armoured tanks. Once inside the gated City Centre—from Boots to Marks & Spencer—security guards stood at doorways demanding, with a casual nod of the head, all incoming shoppers open up their bags and purses for inspection. Would it be that easy to find a bomb, I wondered? Despite the hostility of these daily intrusions, locals took them with ease. They had become a way of life.

Mrs. Petty was a widow now and her children grown. "They've gone away to America," she told me. "One east coast, one west. Makes for a challenge with visits, I tell you. That's why I have them come here."

She ran the farm with the help of hired men. No cattle or horses, just sheep. Chickens clucked around the gravel driveway. I'd seen her tossing them feed. She was always doing something. "Stop and that's when the mischief comes in." So I knew she didn't believe in poetry. She was a businesswoman underneath that housewife demeanor. She liked that I paid a good sum for rent. Having the House of Poets here on Islandmagee, an island-that-wasn't-an-island, provided a nice supplement to her tidy income.

Welcome to Loyalist Larne, read the sign on a brick wall. The image of a man with long curly white hair sitting on an upright horse, as if ready to charge into fight, was saturated with primary colours. In-your-face colours.

"That's King Billy," she said.

I looked down at the curbstones painted in patterns of red and bright blue. "No orange and green here," she said proudly.

You mean no Catholics, I wanted to say.

Mrs. Petty, like most residents of Islandmagee (except Benny and Janet), went to church on Sundays: Presbyterian, like Nana Florence's church in Owen Sound. God was something to fight over, claim. I looked up. Rays of light poked through the clouds like strings from an instrument. But who was playing whom?

Good fences make good neighbors, wrote Frost. But that only worked when both sides were content with their territory. Power was King, not God. More was better, always.

I thought of a dog marking its territory with drips of blue and red paint. The visual stench of it. *Beware. You're not wanted here.*

"Who was King Billy?"

"Goes back to 1690, the Battle of the Boyne." She turned into a parking lot and headed to a block of tall elms. "My secret spot," she said, switching off the engine.

I waited for her to say more but she didn't. She pulled some thick plastic bags out of the boot and saw me eyeing them. "To put the messages in." She handed me one.

Messages meant "groceries"; I knew that now. The meaning had revealed itself, finally. I was learning to wait for the revelation of things.

Patience and timing, Mom used to say, sewing quilts and crafts in her corner nook. To ask was to admit weakness, vulnerability. I didn't want Mrs. Petty to know what I didn't.

I decided not to go to the Co-op first. I didn't want her eyeing my "messages." I went to the drugstore instead—the "chemist"—to buy toiletries and tampons. The shelves were crammed with brand names I didn't recognize, but eventually I found what I needed.

Outside the shop, I was about to turn right but something pulled me the other way. I headed through a low-lit tunnel and once through the narrowing passageway, I discovered kiosks selling items not found in bigger shops. Candles. Knicknacks. Crafts. The one selling jewellery caught my eye.

The pieces on display were modern and stylish with an uncanny quality, as if I'd seen them before (but where?). I fingered a heart-shaped necklace and while doing so, I realized it wasn't one heart but three. They were layered like plates—small, medium, and large—joined by a knotted black cord. Tiny holes were drilled into each to link them as one. Pink, then blue, and the largest—slate grey—was almost black.

"Feel free to try it on," said the store clerk. Her blonde hair was bunched on top of her head like cotton candy; I could feel its stickiness like heat. She held up an oval mirror.

I slipped the knotted black cord over my head. The hearts were cold on my skin, a soft *clacking* when I let go. "Little nests," I said, gazing at my reflection. For a moment I forgot she was there. I usually avoided trying things on in public. I needed to hide to see.

"It's the only one, and oh, it looks brilliant on you. Where you from?"

"Canada."

"You seemed too nice."

I smiled. "I'll take it."

She tucked the necklace into a small brown bag.

"Enjoy the trinity," she said.

On the drive back to Islandmagee I noticed a solitary tree in the middle of a field; a pile of stones surrounded its base.

"It's a fairy tree," Mrs. Petty said.

"A what?"

"It's for the we folk. Many believe in them. Can't say I do. But don't ask me to be the one to chop it down."

The "we" folk. Ah, "wee." A wee cup of tea. But the amount was the same, below the rim.

"What's there to believe?" I was curious to know the magic.

"It's the entrance to the otherworld. To cut down a fairy tree is to bring bad luck. Even to touch one, well, why would you want to go and touch a tree in a field? Unless you were a bit daft."

"It doesn't seem practical leaving it there." The people of Islandmagee—Protestants from what I could tell—were the no-nonsense type. Clearly, some superstitions lingered.

"Andy Evans wrote about them. Or was it Benny? Maybe both. It's the real estate of the poet, if you ask me. Fairies."

Off with the fairies, I'd heard people say, rolling their eyes.

"That fancy car manufacturer, DeLorean, chopped one down outside Belfast to build his automobile factory." She smirked. "The place didn't last. Brought on his own demise, so he did."

"It's hawthorn, right? We had them at the quarry." Springtime they blossomed pure white but the branches were studded with thorns. I had to dodge them while cutting grass with Dad's push lawnmower. Sometimes a miscalculation led to scrapes.

"I've touched them," I said.

She pulled into the gravel driveway and looked at me. "Well, aren't you the one, then."

I refused to believe in superstitions. Black cat crossing a road. Walking under a ladder. And who ever cracked a mirror and got seven years of bad luck? Unless you threw something at it, something I wanted to do as a teenager, brush in hand, staring at the face staring back at me—I looked nothing like the images in *Teen* or *Seventeen Magazine.* I was the opposite of pretty.

Step on a crack and break your mother's back. But I did, many times. I should've been more careful as a little girl.

The second year of my psychology degree I took an operant conditioning class. My assigned pigeon Red had learned a little dance—turn this way and peck a green key, turn the other way and peck a red key; only then did she receive a food pellet. I trained her into this superstitious display by flicking keys and providing pellets to give her the illusion of control. I shaped my bird into that odd behaviour. I made the dance happen.

One spring day while walking home from school I veered off our long gravel driveway towards the quarry to pick some white blooms and a thorn cut me. I sucked the blood until it went away.

Fairy tree. I liked the thought of something poised between the Otherworld and this one—a gateway into the wee-people realm. And I liked that the tree was solitary. This logic made sense to my grief. And whether or not you believed in the fairy realm, a tree was saved.

We never asked about Andy Evans again. We moved into our own group dynamic with Benny and Janet. My "Fire" poem fell flat with the group.

"Aren't fires crackling?" Iris said. She flicked back her thinning hair.

"You need some onomatopoeia," said Declan.

The Americans agreed. But Benny liked it. He said the subdued soundscape that wove through each stanza magnified the grief:

> *Who will know I'm here?*
> *Who will know I've gone?*

We sat in the seats we always sat in, a scatter of wicker chairs and one sofa. I had the best view. I could see—on the other side of the Petty farmhouse—a small island called Muck. *Muck* meant "pig" in Scots Gaelic. The view from the House of Poets provided the perfect vantage point to trace its outline—rock-tail on one end, rock-snout the other, and a long flat back of emerald green. Above it flew a halo of birds—flying, landing, flying again.

The Pettys once owned the tiny island, but after her husband died, Mrs. Petty sold it to the Northern Ireland Nature Authorities as a way to honour him. The Nicholas Petty Bird Sanctuary. But nobody called it that. The name *Muck* stuck.

"The music room" was the designation Benny gave to the location where we now sat. Its stacks of old record albums and outdated record player crammed in the corner (no boombox here), were they the reason? Or maybe the moniker was Benny's way to help us mine the music in our words.

In addition to poetry, Benny wrote song lyrics. During morning break, lunch hour, pre-dinner, post-dinner—anytime at all—he pulled out his beige, battered guitar and began strumming. Whenever he played those first few notes, no matter what Janet was doing—cooking, pouring herself another gin and tonic, pouring Benny another neat whiskey—she stopped to say, "That's my Benny."

When today's workshop ended, everyone left the room except Beth. She had this habit of twirling her long brown hair into a chignon and holding it there before letting it go, only to start all over again. She did this whenever a workshop wasn't going her way, and today hadn't. "What the hell matters in this poem of yours?" Benny had said, running his hand through his hair, the grey curls bouncing back into shape each time. "Bric-a-brac, I tell you. Sounds like a poem. Looks like a poem." He flicked his fingers in the air. "Poof! Bloody air."

Beth's jaw moved in and out when he said those words. She could handle it, couldn't she? The tough boxy-shaped American from New England stock?

"Benny's right," said Janet, standing at the doorway. She was always appearing and disappearing. "You need to step up your game."

But his comments towards me had shown otherwise. I was already in the game. I just needed to keep going.

Beth stared at my necklace.

I touched the three hearts as if to protect them.

"I suppose that's you and your parents," she said.

I looked down to hide my surprise. Me and my parents. Of course, why hadn't I thought of that before? The strange feeling when I first saw it; *the last one*, the shopkeeper had said, *the only one.*

Before my arrival at the House of Poets, there were nightly parties. Declan and Iris referred to them often. They were happy to remind me and the two Americans of our missing out. The events carried their own rhythm—morning workshop, an afternoon poetry talk by the visiting poet, evening readings. And then—

"One night Burly Connors was so hammered, he took a leak out the front door," Declan said. "Waved his penis all over the place and Benny shouting, 'Show us your wee mawn, Burly!' One of the neighbours called the peelers. She said her visiting granddaughter was *traumatized* by the 'little pink snake poking out of the bald man's trousers.'"

Burly Connors. Sean Hamus. Mary Ann Byrne. I recognized the names from the anthology I'd purchased back in Canada, *The Penguin Book of Contemporary Irish Poetry.* Benny's poems were there too but not Janet's.

After today's lecture on Yeats, we piled into Iris's Saab and headed to the nearest pub. Sitting at a round table, we sipped our pints.

"Embarrassing," Beth said. "All Benny did was read a few of Yeats's poems and strum his guitar again: *Like a long-legged fly upon the stream / her mind moves upon silence.*" Her exaggerated tone made us laugh. Even Iris, who rarely smiled, joined in. "And you know," she continued, "his 'wee cup of tea' is spiked."

"No!" said Helen.

Iris nodded. "Janet, too. She's all about the gin."

"*We* could teach better," Declan said. "I mean, I read *Autumn Journal* years ago. What new insights did Janet bring on MacNeice's work last week?"

"Maybe that's what we're supposed to do," Helen said. "Bring in new insights."

"Speaking of insights," Beth said, looking at me. "I hear you don't have to write an academic paper." She eyed the others. "Nice for some, *eh*, like they say in Canada."

"Really?" said Iris, watching me. "I thought writing poems was hard, the paper's brutal."

I sipped my Tennant's to loosen the tightness in my throat. "I didn't get out of it. I still have to write one—a personal essay—"

"Without footnotes and academic rigor." Beth smirked. "Sounds like memoir to me. Sure, they see you as family now. Living so close, you're there all the time. I don't know how you do it." Flipping her hair, she glanced out the window then looked at me. She smiled. "I'd be bored out of my mind here. Who knows what I'd do."

I held her gaze and tried not to blink.

"At least there's life in Belfast," she said.

Beth's comments were still buzzing through me the next day like flies that needed swatting. I put down my notebook and peered out the cottage window at the gauzy sun. If I went out for a run now, I'd catch the remaining light. I changed into my running gear, grabbed my Walkman, and headed out.

Bedsheets blew in the wind like sails going nowhere. *I am going somewhere*, I told myself as I passed Mrs. Petty's clothesline and began a gentle jog. Dodging potholes, I headed up the zig-zag lane, away from the House of Poets, the farmhouse, away from Portmuck Harbour, my heart pumping hard, and when I reached the hilltop, only then did I let myself turn to look back.

There's nothing for you here.

"You're wrong," I said and began running. Bursts of wind pushed in gentle slaps. At least something was touching me. I turned up the music full blast before racing around the corner.

Shit!

A blue car screeched to a halt and a dark-haired, fine-boned woman charged out of it. "My God, you okay?"

It was hard to stand up. I wobbled as I rose out of the prickly hedge.

A curly-haired girl, a bit older than my Grade Three students, stared from the passenger seat. Another girl with much shorter curls sat strapped in a car seat in the back, sucking a soother, her eyes wide and watchful.

"You're one of the students," said the woman.

I nodded. I couldn't talk. I needed to regain my composure from the dizzying sensation. There were scratches on my hands and neck, but thankfully no pain.

"Can I give you a tip?" She pointed to my headphones, dangling at my waist. The song drifted up: *What is love? Baby don't hurt me…*

"Oh," I said, pressing the stop button. "Of course."

"You scared me and my girls," she said. "Don't do that again."

Intuition is part of the creative process, and to help access mine I used the Inner Child Tarot cards Linda had given me before I left for Northern Ireland. Other than Aunt Doris, she was my closest tie to Dad. We were alike in many ways, though she was more big sister than pseudo-stepmother. Linda knew, as my aunt knew, given Dad's controlling nature, he would never have let me come here.

The major arcana were derived from fables and fairy tales such as "The Emperor's New Clothes," *Peter Pan*, and *The Wizard of Oz,* my favourite.

My nerves were still tender from the near accident. I opened the pack and started shuffling.

I chose the three-card layout—past, present, and future—and fanned them on the floor in front of the freshly-lit fire. Before picking each card, I thought hard about the time frame.

Past.

First House: Ten of Crystals.

Stockings hung by a fire. It was the season Mom loved most. "Fire" like my recent poem, a nice connection. A little girl, stretched out on a rainbow-coloured carpet, was holding a crown like the one I used to make from tinfoil sheets when playing "Princess" as a little girl.

Caitlin, the Princess.

Present.

Corner House: Ten of Wands.

On this card a girl was immersed in nature: birds, birch trees, butterflies. She had wings.

Future.

Home Around the Corner: Child of Swords / Pinocchio.

Pinocchio (without a long nose) stares into a mirror and his features reflect back with a long, pointed nose. A candle burns beside him, dangerously close; it could scorch him at any moment, but a series of tools are within reach—sword, hammer, and nails—to help solve any problem. A goldfish in a glass bowl rises to the top.

You are asked to investigate the power of truth in your life. How honest are you?

In the realm of the psyche, whosoever controls the traditional metaphor also governs the mind.

The ancients referred to the trinity as a system of thesis, antithesis, and synthesis.

None of this made sense. I tucked the cards back in the box and went to bed.

I never saw Dad's Caddy again. The car was impounded after the accident. But I saw the deer he swerved to miss that night in a recurring dream. Its frozen, leggy stance, locked in headlights, became my frozen stance—my feet, hooves, my head, heavy with antlers.

I jolted out of the vision.

"This is crazy," I said to the cottage walls. Too white. They needed colour.

I got up from the sofa—my neck tight from the awkward position I'd dozed off into—and hunted down all the vivid pictures and postcards I could find, started taping them on the cottage walls haphazardly. Ticket stubs from concerts—Petty,

Springsteen, Thompson Twins; my picture of Plath. I even ripped out pages of *Goblin Market.*

No photos of my parents or the quarry. They were inside me.

Stuffed in the drawer I found a course catalogue. *The Education Association: Classes for Everyone!* Quilting, woodworking, curling, literature. I flicked through it and found *Beginner's Guide to Yeats.* An eight-week course taught by poet Andy Evans.

His beard was dark brown like my thesis professor, Dr. Delio, but without the flecks of grey. He was tall, over six foot, but Andy Evans stood sturdier than my father's lanky six-foot-six frame; his legs were like two solid trunks fused at the hip. He wasn't my type so I knew I was safe but when he spoke— the timbre, the tone—I couldn't say what exactly—I found myself startled, pulled in. I shifted in my chair and avoided his eyes. My blood rose in warm blooms.

I was the youngest in the class of five women. We sat around a long table in a room off the gymnasium in the Whitehead Recreational Centre. Whitehead was the tiny seaside town where I caught the train whenever I needed an injection of city life. It too was a distance, always a challenge getting from A to B. The buses in and out of Portmuck were rare and unpredictable, so I was forced to rely on lifts to Whitehead (or anywhere else for that matter)—Mrs. Petty, Janet, or Benny. It made me feel like a child.

We circled around, introducing ourselves. I hated group talk. One-on-one was my preference. I could open up then, become who I really was, even to myself. I'd opened up to Dr. Delio in his third-floor office in the Psychology Building to share my grief. I could sense the undercurrent of unsaid things. With all eyes on me, this disappeared.

"Let me guess," Ruth said, sitting directly across from me. I could tell she'd been beautiful once, but middle age had smeared that. "Canada."

I nodded.

Her eyes were dark like her black-dyed hair.

"Oh, you're good, Ruth." Marion's voice was soft like her eyes. "Andy, did you hear that?"

"There was a rumour of a Canadian running about. The House of Poets, I'm guessing."

"I'm doing the M.A. there." I slipped off my jean jacket.

"So that's why you've come here," Andy said and grinned. He coughed into his cupped hands. "Now, let's get started and let's start big: Yeats. W. B. Sure, we could begin with the twilight years, but why not the epitaph?" He took his seat at the head of the table and passed out handouts. From his reflection in the table's veneer, I knew he was looking at me.

"*Cast a cold Eye / On Life, on Death. / Horseman, pass by!* Hear that? The hard C's?" Andy said. "Alliteration sets off the intensity. Like C-C-Caitlin." He smiled. "But sure, what *is* a cold eye? Anyone?"

"My Granny Mable," Doreen said, "eyeing me when I took a second biscuit from her tin."

We all laughed.

"She was a titch of a woman," Doreen continued, "but oh, what a presence!"

"Yes," Andy nodded, "the eye communicates. But what about the Poet's eye? Why cold?"

"Objectivity," said Ruth.

"Sure, one must have some coldness to be an artist," Andy said. "To shape the emotion. Feelings alone don't make for art."

"I think," said Maureen, "it's all about that little strand of time between life and death. It's all the artist has. *Tempus fugit*. Time's winged chariot won't wait!"

Andy looked around the room. "Any other takers? Caitlin?"

My heart raced with everyone watching me, but I was determined to say something. "Don't tell readers what to think. Let them participate by *feeling* their way through the work. Chekhov talks about that. What's said and what isn't. The fine line between."

"He does," said Andy. "In one of his letters, I believe. There's that famous quote. And sure, he was a doctor, wasn't he? He knew the human heart."

"I don't get the horseman though," Doreen said. Or was that Maureen? The two elderly women across the long table both wore blue sweaters—one mohair, the other wool. They looked like sisters.

"Well," said Andy. "Could the horseman be Death?"

"He's already dead, for God's sake," said Ruth. "You said it was his epitaph."

Andy smiled. "Yes, but the words are for the living. What we encounter when visiting his grave."

"Visiting graves. I've never understood that," said Ruth. "The dead don't give a toss."

I thought of my parents in Owen Sound at Greenwood Cemetery. Mom's name was chiselled on the Maharg family stone but not Dad's. Even though it was his last wish to be buried beside his Rusty, Nana Florence wouldn't give permission. Thankfully, her cold eye (eventually) thawed. His grave was below hers though, a footstone.

"It's the four horsemen," Mary said, "from the Bible, and—"

"There's mystery there too," I said, cutting in. Mary flashed me a look. I couldn't stop. "Like a riddle that can't be solved, and yet we keep trying to solve it. The mystery of life. Of death."

"You're too young to know about death," Ruth said. She pursed her lips.

I sat up as if she'd kicked me.

"Now, now," said Andy. "Let's stick to the words on the page. In fact, turn the page over."

Rustling filled the fluorescent lit room.

"Oh," said Doreen. Or was it Maureen? "I knew it! 'Under Ben Bulben.' That's where the epitaph comes from."

"*Swear by what the sages spoke / Round the Mareotic Lake.* Hear it?" said Andy. "He's setting up the rhyme scheme, the unfolding pattern." As Andy continued reading, the rhythm seeped.

I blurted out, "*On limestone quarried near the spot.*"

"Caitlin?" said Andy.

"I… I grew up by limestone, a quarry—"

"*On limestone quarried near the spot / By his command these words are cut: / Cast a cold eye / On life, on death. / Horseman, pass by!*" Andy said.

"Wait!" said Ruth, flipping the page over and back. "There's punctuation here." She flipped it to Andy's rendering of the epitaph. "None here."

"It changes things, right?" said Andy. "Or does it?"

We thought this through.

"That exclamation point," I said, "is the energy of life. A reminder to keep that cold eye for as long as possible. The absence of punctuation," I looked down to confirm my thoughts, "there, in the epitaph, it's the absence of life. Yeats' words have turned cold like his blood." Where was this coming from? Did it make any sense? I looked at Andy and another thought pushed into my mind: *Alone, I want to be alone with you.*

Andy nodded.

When our time was up we continued to sit under the enchantment Andy had created. I thought back to Benny's class on Yeats. What had I learned? That his poems could be put to music, strummed on a battered beige guitar.

After gathering his knapsack and leather jacket, Andy tucked in his chair as if breaking the spell and we slipped into doing mode: gathering our things, putting on our coats.

The night sky was free from day's earlier rain and the dark air chilled and fresh. Sporadic puddles gleamed from the popping headlights. The taxi stand was to the left of the community centre. Or was it right?

"You heading to Portmuck?" Andy asked me.

"The taxi stand is over—" I pointed to the right.

"No. It's the other way," said Ruth appearing out of the darkness. I thought she'd already driven off. "You need a lift?" she said. "Come with me."

"Sure, that's out of your way," Andy said and looked at me. "You're at the Petty farm, right? I think my wife nearly ran you over."

Wife. Of course he has a wife. I saw the two curly-haired girls looking out from a blue car. I looked beside him. That car.

"Don't you need to get home to your family, Andy?" Ruth said.

Andy opened the passenger door. "Caitlin, hop in. Ruth—how about you stay out of trouble, and we'll see you next week."

As I wedged myself between discarded juice boxes and a naked plastic doll, Andy grabbed its arm and threw it in the back.

Maa-maa.

"Sorry about the mess. You enjoy the class?"

"Very much."

He started the engine. "Good to hear. I get revved up after nights like this." He turned on the headlights. "I could sure use a pint." He looked my way. "You in a hurry to get back?"

"No." Should I have said that?

"The White Cliff's close. Been there?"

"Benny and Janet stopped there once to get a bottle of wine." I remembered thinking: you can't do that in Ontario, buy unopened wine bottles from restaurants and bring them home. "We were sorry you couldn't make it to our workshop. I hope it wasn't something too serious."

"They know you're here?"

"With you?"

"This class. They know you're taking my class?"

"No—not yet."

"Interesting. It will be interesting when they find out."

I didn't know what to make of that. "We were under the impression that you lived far away. But you live here like them."

"Oh, I live here all right. And I've been there."

"The House of Poets?"

He smiled at my puzzled face. "My treat," he said, pulling into the lot of the White Cliff Inn.

The pub was near empty except for two men at the bar. I sat at a corner table and waited as the bartender prepared our pints. Brown liquid quickened down each glass in sluggish strips. After letting the contents settle, he poured more in. A white band formed at the top.

Andy was laughing with the barman. They obviously knew one another. Or did they? Andy was like Dad that way. He had that social ease and could talk to anyone.

"The best sip is the first," he said, returning. We clinked our glasses. What if I didn't like it? Could I tell Andy that?

Smooth and creamy, it tasted like peat. I took another sip before wiping my mouth. "It's good."

Andy smiled. His teeth—white, straight, and lovely.

I looked down at the coaster: *Guinness Is Good for You.*

"You know why it's good? Iron. They served it to mothers in hospital after giving birth."

It was hard to imagine that happening in Canada. Mom guzzling down a pint after birthing me or Nana Florence downing one after birthing Mom—but maybe it did.

"I never went back to the House of Poets," Andy said, "because they never paid me. I gave three workshops there plus a talk on Yeats before you came along. Still waiting for the cheque."

I didn't know what to say. I could see that happening too easily and felt somewhat guilty hearing it.

"Canada. Of all places. What made you come here?"

I thought about telling Andy about my parents but it seemed too soon.

"Poets are born, not made. William Butler Yeats at the House of Poets, can you imagine? But you're here and making the best of things." He grinned.

Andy caught the barman's eye, and he began preparing us fresh pints. "Glad you enjoyed the class. Bottom line is, with poetry every word matters. Every beat. The silence. Especially the silence. Let's say I remove the word 'cold' from Yeats's epitaph. *Cast an eye on life on death horseman pass by.* It just isn't—" He sipped. "Poets work the words in new ways. Like a magician. Remove 'cold' and the line is dead."

We developed a weekly routine. Andy picked me up to take me to class, and after class we went for pints before he drove me home. No naked dolls or discarded juice boxes in the blue car, the interior was always spotless. I lived for Tuesdays, found myself whistling, something I never did, something Dad did those days he was secretly seeing Linda (I see that now), looking dapper in his ivory scarf (never tied, always loose) and camel coat before heading out to "watch a game"—hockey, football, baseball—"with the boys." Mom was alive then, bedridden at home. "Don't you look nice," Nana always said, eyeing him with her blue-saucer eyes. Cold eyes.

Friends, me and Andy. That's what we were.

II

We weren't ready to part, not yet. The night ferries, lit like candlelit cakes, travelled back and forth, from Larne to Stranraer, as if pulled by invisible strings. Wind buffeted the darkness. This inlet of isolated beach became our refuge to do what we could do in sweaters and jackets before the edges we touched made us depart. Browns Bay became our place.

"We need to get away, Cat," Andy said one night.

The plan was to meet at Central Station in Belfast and board a train to Dublin. We would leave from Whitehead but at different times so not to arouse suspicion. Once off an island-that-wasn't-an-island and into a faraway city, we would be safe.

There was so much anticipation running through me as the train rumbled towards the city. My skin radiated heat but when I touched my arm, it felt cold. I was always cold here. Mrs. Petty never put the heat on when driving. Long denim skirt, matching sweater, and paisley headscarf—her attempt at dressing up—what mature woman wore here—purchased, no doubt, from Marks & Spencer. Clothes I would never be caught dead in.

"What should I tell her about going away?" I'd asked Andy.

"It's none of that old biddy's business. You have your own life."

So I told Mrs. Petty a kind of truth. I was heading to Dublin to visit the National Gallery of Ireland. She knew I loved the paintings of Jack B. Yeats. I'd mentioned it during one of our awkward drives into Larne (her silence always made me ramble). Somehow the famous poet's painter brother had transformed primary colours—red, blue, and yellow—through shape and form into grief's viscous weight. Every time I looked at "Grief"—the print hung over the fireplace in the music room at the House of Poets—I saw something new and felt something deeper. But the white horse and rider were there from the start— *Horseman, pass by.*

"I'll give you a lift to Whitehead so you can catch the train." Mrs. Petty had insisted. I could only say yes.

Janet and Benny knew I was taking Andy's course—Beth was only too happy to tell me. "They say you're taking someone else's class," she said one day after workshop. "Who might that be with?"

"A local," I said, determined to withhold his name. She was no longer twirling her mud-brown hair into a chignon. She was shaking it back and forth as if in a tacky shampoo commercial. She was Benny's favourite now. I told myself it didn't matter.

I turned to the train window to savour what was happening inside me—grief loosening at the edges—I could feel the melt. I was wearing my favourite outfit: blue jeans, blue top, both tight.

When the train stopped at Carrickfergus (I'd yet to visit the Norman castle there) a family of four headed my way. The mother—I assume it was the mother—had the same carrot-coloured hair as the baby in her arms. The father, also red-headed, was wearing a Johnny Cash T-shirt. He gripped the wrist of the older red-haired girl and tugged her along.

"Go on," he said, nudging her towards me. "She can sit there, can't she?"

"Yes," I said, sounding like a stranger to myself. I'd been so wrapped in silence and though my mind was always racing, my mouth remained shut. People who live alone often talk to themselves, but that's the old and lonely, like Dad after Mom died. "What was that, Dad?" I'd ask when entering a room. "Nothing," he said. "Just thinking out loud."

I never let on that I knew. He was pretending she was there.

The girl's curls were more auburn than red. The father poked at her playfully and she crouched forward, stifling a giggle. He took up most of the aisle with his bulk. His wife was squeezed against the far window, her youngest attached to her like a pelt.

As a child I wanted to please the adults in my world, especially my parents (most of the time). I enjoyed the sheen of goodness compliance gave. Quiet and nice meant you were a good girl.

We had the quarry then. Forty acres of land with a blue eye in the middle. Oval and open, trees fringing like eyelashes. One afternoon Dad asked me to get him a ruler. I found an old one of mine in his top study drawer—flower-er-marked with magic marker, now faded pink. And then I found something else.

"What you got there?" he said, not looking at the ruler but at the glossy black-and-white photo in my other hand.

I dropped the ruler onto the glass table and it made a chipping sound. Plunking down on the chesterfield, I showed him the photo. "It's us, right?"

Dad looked to the family room ceiling. "The view from above." His voice quivered like a loose string.

"It's what the Great Blue Heron sees during flight or the osprey circling for prey," I said.

He nodded.

Quarry. The core of us.

It was all an illusion. Gazing out the train window, these words rose up: *When we did what we did and the round moon entered and took us in.* I grabbed for my notebook. *Shit.* Was it *took us in* or *took me in*? The auburn-haired girl stared as I faced the blank page.

"Stop watching the nice lady," the father ordered.

She flinched.

"It's okay," I said and gave a forced smile. The father's frown remained.

Sometimes the tension at the quarry grew to an unbearable state. Nana Florence eyeing Dad's every move, the sound of her sucking teeth. Mom in her chesterfield nook smoking cigarette after cigarette, lost behind smoke.

One evening after dinner Dad held up the tea towel I'd left crumpled on the kitchen counter and swung it at my face. "You dried the dishes with this?"

"Yes," I said, grabbing my windbreaker.

"And where do you think you're going?"

"Nowhere!" I said and slammed the door.

It wasn't dark, not yet, and the absence of clouds made the dusk appear brighter. I headed around the carport. Dad's new Caddy sat gleaming blue while Mom's green Malibu was accumulating dust. Nana's Oldsmobile was the same shade as her one gold tooth. The car seats were still covered with the original plastic. Whenever she drove me to school I slid back and forth as if on thin ice.

I kicked at the gravel, and some pinged the Caddy. Dad would freak if I'd scratched it. I didn't check. I headed to the woods.

The loamy smell of things dying grew in strength as I

stomped my own path. There was nothing to pin my anger on. It made me think of that stupid Pin the Tail on the Donkey game. But how can you see when blindfolded? I guess that was the point. But why donkey? Why not horse or bull or cow, chicken, sheep? And did I really want to pin pain onto something?

I heard a rustle from behind. I stopped and hid behind a big maple. Deer? Fox? An escaped mink from the nearby mink farm? Through the antlers of branches I saw a tall figure walking back and forth in a haphazard way. Like someone lost.

"Caitlin? You there?"

Of course he would come looking for me. Deep down, I knew that. He was tied to me. We were tied to each other. Soon it would be just the two of us.

The ticket collector entered our carriage. I had mine at the ready—proof I'd paid. I didn't have to reveal who I was or where I was going. All I had to do was present a ticket.

When the collector passed, the red-headed father stood up and shook his legs—perhaps he had pins and needles. Tucking in his Johnny Cash T-shirt, he sat back down. I smiled. The Man in Black, his face contorted, was flipping the bird.

"Ring of Fire." "Folsom Prison Blues." Songs I knew from childhood—background music that grew into a curtain of song. Until coming here I didn't know "Forty Shades of Green" was written by Cash. I knew the phrase of course, but I thought it was an ancient catch term. Cash, in creating that song, had made the phrase famous. Andy's mother, like many here in Northern Ireland, was a fan of the American country singer. Cash, so Andy said, wrote the song while flying home, back to North America—all those greens below him, seeing green like a bird. I thought of Mom's quilt, all those cut green patches becoming one by her careful stitching. Whenever

Andy mentioned the song he never included the shades, he called it "Forty Greens."

I close my eyes and picture
the emerald of the sea.

And then the train stopped. As I headed up the ramp into Central Station, I thought, *What if he isn't here?* I breathed through the panic, saw strangers coming and going, and there he stood in the back of the coffee shop, wearing his leather jacket and blue jeans, motioning for me to come to him.

The next ticket in my hand was for the express train, no stops. We found seats with a table and sat across from one other, our knapsacks beside us as deterrents. The headrests were high enough to block view of other passengers, and we welcomed the privacy. Only a dull lulling sound of nearby voices entered our cocoon.

I set my hand on the table and Andy set his over mine. "God, you're cold," he said, rubbing them like sticks. I jolted when the train moved. It's then I realized I was traveling backwards. Only Andy saw what we were heading into.

In class I always sat kitty corner to his left. And when he parked the car at Brown's Bay we sat side by side. Here, there was no hiding. His eyes were taking me in. No Guinness to quell my nervousness. *He knows what you look like, silly.* But I couldn't stop the urge to run to the washroom—no, toilet (get it right)—to check my carefully prepared make-up and reapply the peach lip gloss I'd purchased especially for the occasion.

I looked down at my hands covered by his—I could barely see them.

"I can't wait to show you Dublin," he said and smiled. He liked showing me things. A few weeks ago, after class, we drove onto a highway that said "Dual Carriageway." The word *dual* made me think of a prearranged fight over some point of honour. But no, that was *duel*. *Dual* meant "double." Two complementary parts, like co-pilot and pilot. Like me and Andy.

We had to stop going to the White Cliff Inn as the ladies had started going there after class. Ruth, no doubt, leading the pack. That first night she saw us in the back corner, she shouted, "Mind if we join you?" Andy gathered chairs while I escaped to the toilet. I stood in front of the sink, not doing anything but putting in time, when she walked in, her black pumps clicking across the floor tiles. I turned on the tap to make it look like I was there to wash my hands.

"You okay?" she asked.

"Fine," I said and smiled brightly.

That night as Andy drove along the dual carriageway, Belfast Lough glistened in the distance like a piece of fallen night sky. Three tall buildings came into view. They commanded their surroundings, the row-houses they towered over. They made me think of the fairy tree.

Andy exited the dual carriageway and we drove along a road. "Biggest housing estate in Northern Ireland. Rathcoole. Means 'back of the ringfort.' It's where I grew up."

The words *biggest* and *estate* made me think of royalty, but the view here proved otherwise: narrow houses, flags with Union Jacks, sectarian murals on walls.

"In one of the apartment buildings?"

"High-rise, you mean. No, we had a corner terrace. More windows, more light."

The murals were of a darker nature than the ones in Loyalist Larne. Three men in black ski masks, all carrying machine guns, reminded me of the Ku Klux Klan, but I didn't say that.

"If I hadn't gone to Grammar School—thanks to Mr. Nelson, my English teacher… well…"

"Poetry changed my life too," I said and touched his arm.

He drove to a nearby park and stopped beside the dark waters, the chain of lights along the lough winking like stars, like some kind of signal. It's then I told him. Mom's cancer. Dad's car accident. "After the policeman knocked at my bedroom door in the middle of the night and told me, all I could say was: 'My God, I'm all alone—'" I reached into my purse for Kleenex.

"Give me one too, will ya," Andy said, sniffling.

We blew our noses and the horn-like racket played like a bad duet. We laughed and our laughter released more laughs, the uncontrollable kind that must run their course by taking over the body.

When I looked down the train aisle, I saw a bony man pushing a food cart in our direction. He pulled out a can of Guinness.

"They sell beer on trains?"

If Dad had taken a train to Buffalo that night (but there is no train to Buffalo, silly). "Be careful," my therapist had warned me, "don't obsess on what-ifs. Try to focus on what is."

Andy turned to see, and despite his beard, I could tell how firm his profile was. I never liked men with beards before. But no, it was boys with beards I didn't have time for, that peach-fuzz lining the chin and upper lip. Dark-bearded men like Dr. Delio and Andy understood the complexities of life (and death). They were my "what is."

Despite Dr. Delio's bold declaration of love, I never slept with him. My instinct to pull away was some kind of protection. Like the Destroying Angel. Despite its gleaming white beauty, the mushroom encased a toxin that killed. Dr. Delio's advances—despite my need—repelled me in the end. But I missed the emotional closeness, badly.

Andy set one hand beneath his chin and gave me a sideways glance. "Who am I?"

"You."

"Come on, you've seen his face—*a thing of beauty is a joy for ever.* Shave this off," he rubbed his beard, "and I'm him." He smiled. Was he joking?

"Is it Yeats?"

He frowned. "*With beaded bubbles winking at the brim.*"

I still didn't know but smiled.

"Anything from the cart?" said the man, thankfully, standing beside us. Andy reached for his wallet and looked inside. He looked at me.

"No worries," I said, digging into my purse. I passed him the money. "Two Guinness," said Andy. He pocketed the change.

We poured our beers into tall plastic cups. The stout flowed in caramel strips as if from a tap and the white band settled. "The ball bearings make it happen," Andy said. It tasted good going down on an empty stomach. *Guinness is good for you,* I thought, smiling. "You know, before I came to Northern Ireland I thought *Keats* and *Yeats* where pronounced the same way. Like *seats, Keats, Yeats.*" I giggled.

"Crikey," Andy said, not smiling. "You do know nothing." He stood up. "Need to see a man about a horse."

Alone in the cubicle I returned to what he'd just said: *You know nothing.* Or was it: *You know, nothing.* I was new to poetry. Mostly self-taught, with so many pockets of not knowing. He couldn't mean I was stupid. He could have any woman he wanted and he chose me. Like Dr. Delio. Of all the females in that massive lecture hall, I was the one my psychology professor had noticed.

I saw how women looked at Andy, the up-and-down glances of approval and come-hither stares. And when they heard the deep register of his voice—*Oooh, you sound like Liam Neeson!*—they leaned in. But he always left them alone and came back to me.

We walked through Connolly Station, our knapsacks on our back. "Is that Stephen Rea?" I asked Andy. The actor's brown puppy eyes stared our way as he sipped from a Styrofoam cup in the station's coffee shop, his brown hair, long and droopy, unlike Andy's short back and sides. The *Crying Game* star sat alone, nobody pestering him for autographs.

Andy nodded and Stephen nodded back. "We don't bother the famous here. We give them a wide berth. Maybe we'll see Bono later."

"No—"

"If you're good, I'll take you there." He squeezed my arm.

Don't I know you from somewhere—Dad loved it when that happened to him. The Christmas after Mom died we escaped to New York City to avoid the painful memories (Dad's idea). That first night (before Linda "happened" to be in the city) we dined in the theatre district. Would we see a star?

"That's George Hamilton," Dad said, giving the tanned, grey-haired man a nod. George returned the recognition.

"You know him?!" I said. I thought of Dad's obsession with sun tanning.

Dad fanned his serviette onto his lap. "I do now."

As we made our way out of the train station's metal-clanging dark, we entered into the bright day. Dublin was wired with energy. Honking cars, lilting voices, people of all ages moving in every direction—by foot, bus, car, bike—to wherever they needed to be.

"You don't mind walking, do you?" Andy asked.

I didn't mind. No armed guards at shop doorways checking purses and bags for weapons or bombs, no passing tanks. There was a freedom here not felt in the North, a sensation like a spring uncoiling. Despite the smell of fumes from passing vehicles, I felt my lungs expanding. Hiding our relationship had taken its toll. In Canada I would never sleep with a married man. But here in the land of forty greens—

I can't do this, I wrote in my journal before agreeing to this trip. Sitting in the white-walled cottage, walls now plastered with colour, I listened to the harsh rush of the sea, the smash of the waves against the L-shaped pier before they fizzled in slow-foam retreat. When I underscored the word *can't,* my pen slipped. It obstructed like a fence. I stared and stared and then scratched in angry lines until the word was buried with ink.

We headed toward a river. "The Liffey," Andy said. He told me the name "Dublin" came from the Vikings. *Dubh Linn,* meaning: Black Pool. I thought of the game Telephone—a phrase, passed on with a cupped whisper, morphs its way down the listening chain to become something else, proof the spoken word was merely jumbled air and inaccurate as gossip.

Andy pointed to another bridge packed only with pedestrians. It made me think of the Bridge of Sighs. I wanted to tell Andy that. I don't know why I didn't. I don't know why I wanted to.

Through pedestrian-only Grafton Street we squeezed between the determined shoppers heading to Bewley's, Brown's, or Boots and circled the crowd that had gathered around the guitar-strumming busker, singing—so Andy said—"Molly Malone," the statue we'd just passed of a woman with ample breasts (her dress barely contained them) behind her cart of wares.

Crying, "Cockles and mussels, alive, alive, oh."

We approached a stone archway that led to St. Stephen's Green. "Over twenty acres in there."

"The quarry was over forty," I said. "Water, plus all the land around it."

"So you had double then. Servants too?"

"No. Of course not."

Did he think I came from money? We had a lovely home beside the quarry, a cedar-walled bungalow, but it was modest in size. Yes, I had my own bedroom and adjoining bathroom, as did my parents—plenty of space for the three of us—and the third bedroom that served as Mom's sewing room, before she got too sick, became Nana's room when she arrived to help out. "Temporary," Dad said. Later I would learn *temporary* meant "until your mother dies." No one mentioned the word *death*. It was as abstract as romantic love.

But the previous owners did have a servant. That room became Dad's study. And yes, it had a side entrance door.

Not my fault.

Andy was raised in a small house, sure, but he had a family—a younger brother, a mother and father (though now divorced), and now his own children (I didn't want to think about that). And for adventures in nature—what I had at the quarry by stepping out the bungalow door—he and his mates simply boarded a city bus to the Mourne Mountains, where they camped out overnight in Tullymore—a tent near the river—reading Thoreau's *Walden* and Wordsworth's *The Prelude* aloud. Andy knew where to go to find what he needed, away from the confines of Rathcoole's concrete.

"Some of the Easter Rising happened in that park. Not just the Post Office like I showed you. Now, here's something people don't know. During fighting, they halted their gunfire so the groundsman could go in and feed the ducks in the pond."

"I love that," I said, imagining it.

That first year at the quarry, Mom and Dad surprised me with a gift of six ducklings. Their downy feathers were as soft as a stuffed toy. The chicken wire pen we kept them in at night was made by one of the hired hands who worked at the nearby mink farm. Daytime, the ducklings paddled around the quarry in a swift yellow pack, darting here and there as one unit. (How did they know to move all at once? What signal was I missing?) Nighttime they slept in the pen; the ground beneath it was sandy, no limestone rocks. I was asleep at the time—or was I?—but the cries, avian screams—the next morning my parents told me. "We're sorry…" I never saw their bodies, some half eaten, I assumed—heads and legs and webbed feet dismembered. My parents couldn't hide the scattered feathers. You'd think there'd been a pillow fight if not for the patches of blood.

We made our way past the city park and approached a series of townhouses with stairs that led to painted doors: red, blue, and yellow like Jack B. Yeats's painting "Grief." Stately and orderly homes. Andy said it was the Georgian style.

"What if every door in the world had bright colours?" But he didn't hear me. He was watching an attractive woman with straight dark hair walking towards us. My heart stopped as if a vice had gripped it. She did look like his wife. Giving me a dismissive look, she held Andy's gaze. I could see it wasn't her, her eyes were too close. Could it be a sister or cousin? We were off the island-that-wasn't-an-island, but we were still on the same patch of land anchored in the Atlantic, only two hours or so away. Would we get caught before we started? What was I thinking? We had kissed and touched but not—

Prude. You can't even say the word.

I pulled at the edge of Andy's leather jacket. "Is it—?"

"Time for a jar?" He smacked his lips and eyed the building across the street. The Baggot Inn.

She was nobody, that woman. Relief filtered through me.

I followed him into the hops-smelling darkness, the air thick and clingy with cigarette smoke. It was a place of timelessness, where past and present accumulated into a never-ending now. As my eyes slowly adjusted, more came into view—a jukebox jammed in the corner, signs on walls—"Guinness is Good for You!"—and three tweed-capped men sitting on stools, staring at us.

"All right, boy," said the middle one, nodding at Andy.

Andy pointed to a table near the back. "I'll get us the black stuff." He headed to the bar. I knew not to sit facing the door we'd just walked through, Andy's spot for surveillance, what the Troubles did to him, always on guard for the unexpected—bombs and shootings. I thought back to that first time he crouched beside his parked car. We'd stopped at a pub off the Antrim Coast after his night class in Glenarm. He was wary about going in and didn't relax even after two quick pints. The men in the pub kept eyeing him. "Let's go," he said, though I hadn't finished mine. I followed him out in a scurry. When he stopped, I stopped. To my surprise he dropped on all fours and looked under the Astra. "Andy?" I said, puzzled. Was a cat hiding there? After a solid check he stood back up and wiped his hands on his jeans. "Don't just stand there," he said, his eyes accusing. His tension buzzed through me. Only after we drove away and were along the coastal road—the star-drizzled sky, the glens, and the sea— did he relax. He took a deep breath. "My sixth sense was up with that place." He shook his head. "Shouldn't've stopped, but we're safe." I realized then it wasn't a cat he was looking for. He was checking for bombs.

Daylight streamed through the pub's front window into a glistening block. Passing cars sun-shimmered, as did the people toing and froing. A dog tied to a post wagged his tail at the sight of his owner returning, his black fur glossy with light. Andy, his back to me, continued chatting to the barman. I imagined tracing the wide pathway across his broad shoulders, running my hands down his narrowing back, loosening the taut energy trapped inside those muscles. He was saying something I couldn't hear. The barman smiled. His teeth— yellow and crooked like a fence too damaged for fixing.

Andy's easy manner, the way he made people laugh, yes, it was familiar. But was that wrong? The cancer that had gnawed at Mom's athletic body the years I was growing into mine couldn't obliterate her spirit, her optimistic eye. She fought hard to keep going. Dad gave me the attention she couldn't. After she died I became his emotional mirror. He needed me to be seen. Andy reminded me so much of him.

He set down our drinks. "Nothing like where it's made. The best."

It looked creamier but I couldn't taste any difference. I sipped it again. Perhaps I wasn't trying hard enough. When someone tells you what to expect, there's no room for discovery.

He slipped off his leather jacket and eyed the jukebox. He reached into his jeans' pocket.

I dug out coins from my purse. "Will these work?"

Music was a part of my aural landscape growing up but only when Dad was in the house. He always had the radio on—CBC or that Buffalo station The Music of Your Life. It wasn't the music of *my* life: Crosby, Sinatra, Fitzgerald. Every time the broadcaster announced: *You're listening to*—I was reminded of my annoyance.

Songs the station played brought tears to Dad's eyes when he became a widower, but he refused to stop listening. He didn't hide from his emotions the way Mom did. She preferred silence in the house.

Nana Florence (so the story went) went days and days without talking to her daughter when they lived in the red-brick house in Owen Sound. Mary Ellen (Florence refused to call her daughter "Rusty," the name Mom preferred) became a nobody, a ghost. Simple requests like "What's the time, mother?" or "Pass the salt" were ignored. Florence continued to do whatever it was she was doing: mopping, dusting, darning, cooking, baking, eating, staring through a red-headed girl's tender frame towards a future without her.

Was Mom's silence her way of owning the abuse? Or was she wrapping herself up in self-punishment because deep down, she believed she deserved it?

Andy looked pleased with his song choices when he returned. The first record clicked into place. "Raglan Road" by Van Morrison filled the low-lit room.

We headed up a walkway toward a Georgian building with a bright yellow door. Andy slipped off his wedding ring and tucked it inside the pocket of his knapsack. I didn't let on that I saw.

It was the time I loved most: dusk, the darkest part of twilight. That in-between state when time opened, as if anything could happen.

A grey-haired man greeted us at the door; we didn't have to knock. He eyed me closely and checked my left hand. Prickles travelled down my spine. Was I turning red? I avoided the intruding full-length mirror and watched Andy sign us in.

"Welcome to St. Jude's," said the man, "the Saint of Lost Causes." He eyed me again, this grey-haired man with a bit of a stoop. *I know what you're about.*

"Cat?" Andy said, eyeing my purse. I handed him my credit card.

With our knapsacks on our backs, we headed up the wide set of stairs, carpeted with an exuberant floral pattern, and found our room: number three. The door was ajar so Andy pushed it with his foot and we walked in. That same floral pattern was in our room too—yellows, mauves, and pinks—too feminine to be chosen by Mr. St. Jude so there must be a Mrs. A single red rose sat in a vase on the vanity table. Fully open, its unfolding complete. Soon the softened petals would separate and wither. When I moved closer, it had no smell.

"Jesus, it's like a girl's room," Andy said.

"You're sure it's this one?" I eyed the twin beds and set my knapsack beside Andy's.

"The only room left." He pushed the closest twin toward the other.

We were in the moment we'd wanted but it didn't feel natural. The pints, despite their potency, weren't easing the tension like I'd hoped. This urge to flee grew inside me. I shuffled back and forth to give it a way out.

Through the half-curtained window the night was black-thickening. I wanted the sky to return to the in-between state, the colour in the painting that hung on the far wall—a vivid violet.

"We need music," Andy said, closing the door, locking it. He grabbed the remote and found the music channel, ABBA's "Waterloo" in mid-song. "Bloody shite," he said, turning it off. I didn't say I liked it.

Sitting down on the bed, he patted the emptiness. I sat so our knees were touching. This dissipated the urge to run—it closed the gap. Andy leaned closer. I could smell his citrus shampoo. He took hold of my wrist, his hand like a clasp.

"Wait," he said and flicked off the bedside lamp. The room's darkness highlighted the streetlight's orange glow. When I closed my eyes, his mouth sealed mine, our limbs entangled—hands wandered beneath clothes to skin, to the places lovers go.

"Ah, Lazarus has risen," said Mr. St. Jude when we appeared for a late breakfast. All tables were cleared of place settings except for one. The grey-haired man's prolonged stare didn't bother me this morning. I was flushed for a different reason and he knew it. I picked up a spoon and smiled into it. We'd been two spoons just moments ago as the mourning doves cooed us awake.

After taking our orders, he brought us milky teas. We sipped inside the glow of ourselves, my body alive from Andy's touch—the ease with which we'd given ourselves, the slow moans of *yes*. And I thought of the woman with the perfect surname: Bloom. To flower into a perfume of pink petals fleshy and smooth from human oils moist like tongues open to sun all perfume yes and his heart was going like mad and yes I said yes I will Yes.

She listened to her body. She let it ride her to yes, like we did last night, this morning.

I hadn't realized I was hungry until I breathed in the sinful goods of grease and butter he set before us. I forked the yolk and yellow streamed across the fried tomato and fried potato bread, a silken trail of *yes*.

We sat and ate. Our eyes, when they met over the clink of polished cutlery, said all that was needed.

Once outside the B & B, the sun mirrored our mood. The wind didn't whip away at my body the way it did at Islandmagee. Rarely did it lie dormant there. In Dublin the energy came from the crowds. Making our way into the city centre, I could sense the relaxed atmosphere from the way people moved. In Belfast, when pedestrians walked towards me, they kept firmly on their path. I had to move out of their way.

A whole day before us. Not slivers of minutes between classes and car trips. The steady click of Andy's steel-heeled brogues caught our rhythm as we walked by more houses with brightly coloured doors and more leafy-lined streets like Raglan Road.

Andy stopped in front of a shop window. A taxidermy doe—my totem animal—stood on a wooden platform. *You look like a deer in headlights*. What people said in Canada. It was the animal Dad swerved to miss that night on Stonemill Road, one road from home, and Andy knew that.

I touched my neck. I'd meant to wear the necklace. I felt bare without it.

"We'll see the Yeats, but I want to show you something first."

"Let me guess: a bookstore."

We'd never been in one together. Waterstone's in Belfast was too risky. One day after Andy's trip into the city—he was interviewed on radio again—"It's all happening, Cat. Since I met you…" he told me he'd bookmarked a page in the *Collected Yeats*. "Look for the ink dots in the margin."

The next day when I found it, I saw three barely-there dots beside the last three lines of "He Wishes for the Cloths of Heaven."

But I, being poor, have only my dreams;
I have spread my dreams under your feet;
Tread softly because you tread on my dreams.

We moved as one unit down a grassy path that led to a narrow canal, though I could barely match his long strides. What did he want to show me? I was thinking this when we heard the splash. From the water, a panicked cry. A woman was trying to dog-paddle to the other side. Stepping forward, without a word between us, we leaned down in clock-work unison and each grabbed hold of an arm to lift her out.

She shook like a soggy dog, her sprays pinging us like rain.

"Are you okay?" we asked.

"Oui!" she said, pulling away from us. "Non!"

Her pale sweater and dark trousers dripped with canal water. She looked like she'd just woken up from a dream and we were the culprits who'd snapped her out of sleep. Stepping out of her wet circle, she mumbled incoherently, away from us, the pull of our hands.

I stared at the wet imprint on the patch of cement. It all felt unreal.

"We just saved a woman from drowning," Andy said.

"Should we stop her?"

When we looked again, she was gone.

I followed him across the canal's narrow walkway, the planks responding to our weight, and when I reached the middle, I looked down. The water, falling steadily in three sections, filled the air with white noise. For a moment I thought I saw the woman's legs, dangling there in the splashes. I thought of that painting with Icarus—his pale legs poking out of the water were the only evidence of his fall and no one aware of it happening.

A chill passed through me. Andy stood waiting on the other side.

"I just remembered your dream," I said. A woman in Andy's dream had turned into a dog after falling into a deep pit of water.

He nodded.

"Was it me?" I'd asked for some strange reason. Was I back at the quarry?

"No, but she was crying out your name."

"Really? Cat? Caitlin?" It seemed important to know.

"What is this, the inquisition? I thought you'd appreciate—"

"I do. Of course I do."

"You're inside me, Cat." He'd reached for my hand. "I'm in love with you."

If he hadn't said those words, would we have kept those twin beds separated last night?

Two shadows with their own will, seeking dim light.

Andy took my hand and led me to a nearby park bench. A statue of a life-sized man sitting cross-legged and cross-armed—his glasses wide-rimmed, his hat set respectfully beside him—faced the canal.

"That's who wrote 'Raglan Road,'" said Andy.

"Not Van?" I thought of the song.

"Patrick Kavanagh."

The bronze shape, given its human form, made some buried part of me think it was real and I was invading its space as I sat down beside it. Or was it invading mine? I took a deep breath. The feeling grew. *You're too close*, it said.

And then I remembered a phrase from Kavanagh's poem about this very canal. *Niagarously roaring.* The comparison seemed comical given the canal's size. Clearly, Kavanagh had never experienced the *real* Niagara, a place I knew well from selling bus tours there each summer during university. If that woman had fallen into one of the wonders of the world, it would have been her end.

Kavanagh's "Grand Canal" wouldn't be so *grand* next to the Welland Canal either. Nana Florence's husband—Roderick Maharg, my grandfather—captained lakers through it. Away months on end until the lake ice froze, he transported grain, iron ore, and other commodities to port cities. Thanks to a man-made route that joined the two Great Lakes—Erie with Ontario—the impossible was possible.

A gull landed near my feet. Flapping madly, it squawked a crying laugh.

Niagarously roaring. Who was I to judge? Kavanagh had the right to make those words fit and slip into place the way all myths do, out of thin air and into our hearts, the airy twist through the physical.

We left the canal renewed. As if saving a woman from drowning had given us permission to be together. I thought of the woman who drowned in the quarry. The weight was already inside her body, her soul, her heart, so the rocks she gathered and carried to the water's edge felt light, like the woman we lifted out, a bar of light.

I stared at "Grief." The painting's thick, textured strokes clashed with primary colours, turning the scene into pain.

Navy beneath black, orange-clotted red, gangrene yellow, and fierce blues pushed the eye inward towards black grief. Viewing the original intensified the experience. I shivered.

And I remembered the rabbits. We lived in Grimsby then, no quarry yet. It was spring and I could feel the air opening as I skipped rope. The sudden cut of Dad's lawnmower caught my attention. Crouching, he peered at the grass. Something was there. I ran to see.

"Look," he said, fingering back the grassy lid.

A nest of pink squirms, their eyes sealed shut. I put out my hand—

"Don't—" he said, covering them up. "The mother will know."

A few days later I was ordered to stay inside. I heard panic in my parents' voices even though they were trying to hide it. I peeked from behind my bedroom curtain and saw them scooping limp forms with garden trowels, one after another, strewn across the lawn, dropping them into a plastic bag, wide like a mouth.

The space inside me that felt things, that held my lies, sprung open and shouted: *You touched it!*

Andy's voice made me jump. When I turned to say *Pardon?* I realized he wasn't talking to me. Petite and curvy, compared to me with my long bones, her hair glossy blonde. She was smiling at him, her chin a-tilt, and he was smiling at her, the smile I knew.

"Who was that?" I asked when she left the room.

He avoided my eyes.

I stared back at "Grief."

"Okay," he said, touching my arm. "A friend of Mira's, an old friend. They took drama together."

"I didn't know Mira was an actress."

"Fine little actress."

Was he being sarcastic?

"Accepted to LAMDA." He looked at the floor. "Not my fault she didn't pursue it."

We got ready for bed when we made it back to the room, too tired for anything but sleep. Andy walked around while brushing his teeth. He didn't stay locked in the toilet like I did. I wondered what other habits I'd discover. After pushing the twins together—the chambermaid having separated them (or was it Mr. St. Jude?)—we released the tucked-in sheets and slid in.

Nestled like spoons, his chest hairs tickled my back, his beard bristled my neck. I was a fold of flesh in his hands, a curved accordion. We drifted off.

But my dream turned restless. I was back at the quarry, watching an onset of darkening clouds, and one fingered into a funnel. The sky purpled to ripe green, a bruised light. I raced from room to room, looking for something—I didn't know what—the inside air fusing to black, caged, still.

He woke up hard. I felt him from behind. He wanted in. I wasn't ready. I needed to pee and freshen up and there was too much daylight in the room and the mourning doves weren't cooing yet. He kissed my neck, my shoulders, and turned me over. I lay like a flat blanket, my breasts exposed, his mouth on my nipple, and I jolted.

He pulled away. Sat up as I sat up.

I yanked the bedsheet over my nakedness.

"You think I would hurt you?" he said. Grabbing his clothes, he stomped into the toilet, slamming the door. I could hear the fan whirring.

What just happened?

"Andy?" I said when he finally came out. He was wearing a blue button-down shirt and black jeans. He was dressed for the day.

"You need to get ready," he said. "I'll see you downstairs."

When I went downstairs he was already sitting at our table, facing outward as usual, so I sat facing the wall. Today I had time to see the wall. A red stain on yellow wallpaper, remnants from an uncooperative ketchup bottle, was shaped like a wound. "Lazarus has risen," said Mr. St. Jude when he emerged from the swinging doors. Same joke, same table. But who was he referring to? Me or Andy?

"Same as yesterday," Andy said and grabbed hold of a nearby newspaper.

When our plates arrived I pierced the yolk and watched it spread. The clanking of cutlery was the only sound. Our eyes didn't meet.

"I'm sorry," I said when Andy finally looked at me.

"Not now."

Andy finished his food but I couldn't. There was nothing to do but head back to the room, pack our knapsacks, and depart. I followed him up the stairs and went straight to the toilet to brush my teeth. My breasts were sensitive this time of the month. It happened. I couldn't help it. Why was he punishing me?

It's the end of our time together and he's reacting to it. That must be it. I opened the door.

At first I thought he was gone, but there he was, standing against the wall by the flower painting, the vivid violet. When he saw me see him, he lifted it off and turned it face-down on the unmade bed. He grabbed for a pen and wrote:

A.E.

+

C.M.

Then he circled our initials with a big fat heart before putting it back.

The first picture I ever drew was of a heart. Mom smiled when I showed it to her. She was sitting in the turquoise kitchen, watching the male cardinal dart in and out of the snowy bushes that lined our backyard in Grimsby, the Niagara Escarpment. The heart was lopsided. I frowned. "It's like the real one, Honey," she said, setting it down on the kitchen table, staring at it. She placed my hand over her chest so I could feel the bumpity-bump beating there, below the breast she would one day lose.

I sighed. My relief like a wave. "Andy," I said, moving towards him.

I slowed down my run to take in the view of the rolling green hills that led to Brown's Bay. The ongoing waves crested the sea like a rippling blanket, releasing lines of white foam. The view comforted the way the quarry did when Dad and I sat on the dock to watch the sun lay the day's red blade.

Sweat trickled down my back.

In the end Nana granted Dad's last wish, but he wasn't beside his Rusty. He was beneath her feet, the way Nana always thought of him: beneath. The way she thought of me.

So what? At least she made a concession. It was her family plot after all, and she never let me forget that. In addition to Dad's name, birth and death date, I included another word.

Donald Richard Maharg
beloved of
Mary Ellen Maharg

Wife, husband—they were merely *labels* of love, not love itself. Love was the living feeling that hooked the net of everything.

Mrs. Petty watched me peg another towel onto her clothesline. The chickens gathered in a pecking heap, a feathered scrum, as she tossed out feed. "So, how was Dublin?"

"It was nice," I said, determined not to look at her. I could feel her watchful eyes. I was thankful I had a task to keep me busy.

"And how's yer man?"

My towel fell to the wayside. She knows. Of course she knows. I lifted it back up and told myself to concentrate. I was about to say—What man? You mean Andy, don't you?— but she filled the awkward silence. "Never seen them myself. My life's too busy for art."

The paintings of Jack B. Yeats, of course. *Yer man* was an expression used here. Even Andy said it.

"Intense," I said, thinking back to the weekend. "And beautiful."

I didn't say *confusing*. I wanted to forget that.

She peered into my basket. "You're done," she said. Her blue head scarf rippled in the wind. I'd realized the blue scarf was for working days, the paisley for show. She looked towards the sea. "Sky's clearing. You picked a good day. They'll trap the sun's scent." She looked at her watch. "Time for a cuppa?"

No. I was always saying *no* to her. "I'd love to, but I have to get back to work."

"Yes, work. Seeing yer man tonight?"

I clenched my hands. "You mean night class? Andy?"

"Poor Mira. She almost died, you know. But what a beautiful child, their youngest. Chel they call her. Short for Rachel. A real looker, like her big sister, Grace. They both take after their mother." She clucked at the hens jerking back and forth as if orchestrating them. "You enjoying his classes?"

"I am," I said, turning away from her prying eyes, knowing I'd never be called beautiful yet must be because Andy had chosen me. "They look hungry," I said of the hens. *Like you*, I thought. "He's starting another one."

"*Another* class?"

"In Ballymena, I think."

"Now, that's a fair distance. How will you get there?"

She knew. And she knew I knew that. "Shoo!" I said to the brownish one scurrying towards me. "Andy will pick me up."

"Aye," she said. "Good thing his wife lets him work week-nights. Sure, she hired him, didn't she? Don't know what he does during the day."

He writes poems. Something you're too blind to understand.

You, Mothman, with your wounded wings. Escape the hurtling rocks.

With a line like that you had to know empathy. What it was to be an outsider and suffer.

"Done," I said, grabbing hold of my basket. The hanging towels thwacked in the wind.

The local primary school was close to the red phone box, a space I knew well. Today I didn't enter it to dial the number I knew by heart. Instead I walked past it. Dressed in my ankle-length denim skirt and blue cotton sweater, I looked like Mrs. Petty during her weekly visit to Larne (minus the paisley headscarf). Knowing of my role back home as a primary-school teacher—what I'd left behind, what was waiting for me to return to—she'd arranged for my visit weeks ago.

Growing up I never thought I'd be a teacher. Sure, I played School the odd time as a kid—used a ruler as pointer, checked mock papers, made myself act like I knew what I was doing. It wasn't until I became a T.A. for first-year psych students that I discovered a passion for sharing knowledge—seeing students learn as I learned from them, the growth of the mind.

My original plan after graduation was to pursue a PhD in psychology; the vast number of years it would take became overwhelming when I became an orphan. Teachers' college was one year. To have a pathway set before me helped me manage the grief. Three months before graduation, after my first interview, I was offered a job teaching grade three. Finally, something had gone right.

To hear his voice, to hear what he was thinking. We had a signal for crunch times (ring one, hang up, count to ten, ring again). "*World is suddener than we fancy it.* Beautiful. Isn't it, Cat?" he'd said last night when I called him. He continued, "It made me think of us." Goosebumps slipped down my spine as if MacNeice's title had snowed on my skin. "You need to hear the real stuff. Janet, a poet? Prose chopped up. No depth or musicality. Flat like her Yankee voice. And always about the seals in the harbour."

I stepped through the double glass doors into an empty corridor and entered a tiny office. A fleshy woman with spiky black hair sat planted behind a paper-filled desk chewing her pen cap. She didn't look up. I coughed politely.

"Two doors down. Mr. Pick's expecting you," she said, refusing to look at me.

I approached the half-open door.

"Hello, hello! Welcome!" A short man stood up from his desk and extended his hand. Our handshake moved like a slow-motion saw. "Come in, come in!"

I followed him into the chalk-smelling room.

The students stared from their rows. They weren't arranged into groups like they were in my classroom. Boys in white shirts and navy trousers. Girls in white shirts and navy skirts. I knew which one was his. Even if I hadn't seen her before, I'd know—deep-set eyes, high cheekbones, and her cherry-red lips a rosy contrast to the whiteness of her skin. Her complexion signalled, like his: *I'm alive.* But her hair wasn't dark brown like his or straight like Mira's; it was auburn and curly like mine. For a moment I thought I was looking back at myself, back to a time when I too had parents, a spiral notebook, an eraser-chewed pencil, a Snoopy lunch box.

"I was going to tell them all about you," Mr. Pick said, smoothing his tan trousers, ironing out the creases. "But I don't know a thing." He lifted some index cards from his cluttered desk. "I thought we'd start with questions, so we would. Right, class?" He shuffled the cards. "This is Miss Maharg. She came all the way here to study poetry, so she did. Am I right?" He turned from the eager-eyed students to look at me.

Ms., not Miss. I held my tongue. "And to write poetry."

"Aye, poetry. *To be or not to be.* How 'bout this: To be a bizzzy bee." Mr. Pick chuckled. "We love poetry, don't we, class?"

"Yes, Mr. Pick," said some. Others mouthed the words.

"We hear you're from Canada," blurted a red-headed boy. "Do you know Peter McAllister? He lives in Toron'o."

"Toron'o? Yes. Well, Toronto is a big city. Is he a relative of yours?"

"Cousin. I've only met him once. I wanna go to Toron'o."

"There's a ginormous tower there," said the freckled girl sitting beside him. "I've been up that tower." She looked at the ceiling. "But I was too little to remember. Have you been up that tower, Miss?"

"When it first opened." I smiled. "Long before you were born." Suddenly I felt very old.

"You talk funny," said the squirrel-cheeked boy in the back row.

Mr. Pick laughed. "It's called an accent, Colin. I bet we sound funny to Miss Maharg."

"Call me Caitlin. And yes, I have to admit, you do sound a little funny. Well, did. I'm getting used to it now, so I am."

"A-ha!" Mr. Pick said. "*So I am.* Did you hear that, class? She's one of us."

They smiled and nodded.

"So she is," said Colin.

Everyone laughed, including me.

Andy's daughter raised her hand.

"Yes?" I said.

"What's it like in Canada?"

"Well, Canada's a big country. Second biggest in the world. Let's see… we've got mountains and lakes and rivers and prairies. We're surrounded by ocean on three sides. I live in Ontario, where we have cold cold winters and hot humid summers."

"Is it green like our green?" she asked, twirling an auburn curl.

"In the spring it is."

"Like our forty greens?"

"Well, maybe not as many. But after all the snow's melted and the days have lengthened, things come alive again."

"We have no seasons," said Mr. Pick. "Only spells of sun and rain. The green fades a bit during winter, but it never goes away."

"Do you miss the seasons?"

"Grace," said Mr. Pick. "So many questions." He put down the index cards. "Guess we don't need these."

"I did at first, Grace, but not anymore." I was about to say, *I know your Dad*—I don't know why—when Mr. Pick interrupted.

"We're reading *The Secret Garden*." He looked at his watch. "It's story-time but I must make a trip to the office." He handed me the novel, opened to the bookmarked page. "Do you mind? They can listen to your accent." He hurried towards the open door. "Be good for Miss Maharg, now."

After the bell had gone she came up to me. I was standing in the hallway, looking at the paper-framed family portraits thumb-tacked to the bulletin board, the charcoal sketch of a man with a dark beard. "Mine," she said and skipped down the hall.

The sun warmed my face during my trek up the hill to attend morning classes. *I am the season of buoyancy and aliveness.*

Buds on hedgerows were beginning to emerge. Soon they would bloom into red and purple bells.

The song "Smells Like Teen Spirit" blared from behind along with the rolling motor of a car. The M.A. students—Declan, Helen, and Beth—had bonded further after the shock of Cobain's suicide. The voice of their generation—gone.

I was an 80's girl. Jackson, Madonna, Lauper. "Girls Just Want to Have Fun." Only a small gap between us but one wide enough during the slow-grind days of our youth.

Iris the Mature Student should be the outsider, not me. But I was getting used to it.

Declan leaned his brooding head out the passenger window. "Want a lift?" he said with his lilting accent.

"Very funny," I said and leaned back into the prickly hedgerow to let them pass the short distance. Iris, her hands on the wheel, didn't look my way. Beth and Helen stared from the back with sleep-clouded eyes. None of them had any interest in me. I pretended not to notice. They headed inside the House of Poets.

The sea, from this vantage point, made one giant blue cover, the sunlight made glitter-fields. Nature's quilting. I thought of Mom in her chesterfield nook at the quarry, her legs curled up, sewing quilts and crafts, taking in the watery light.

When I opened the front door, greasy odours wafted out. Janet must have made Benny an Ulster fry again. Fried potato bread, fried mushrooms, fried tomato, fried egg, fried sausage, fried blood pudding and a scoop of baked beans. It was the same breakfast Andy and I had during our time in Dublin, though I could never finish mine. "Heart attack on a plate," Benny said with an impish smile the last time I saw him eating it. He was wearing his terry robe that morning, his long legs exposed, shapely legs though I never saw him exercise. What happened when your M.A. classes took place in someone's home—you saw your instructors in their robes and pyjamas.

Jimjams they called them. Strange at first, this lack of formality and false sense of family, the absence of walls and borders. I'd come up to use the computer in the library that also served as Benny's study, to type and print off some poems for workshop.

Janet looked at the notebook in my hand and checked her watch. "You have time," she said. She knew my routine.

My poems always began in notebook form. I had to feel the ink moving across the page, as if the pen was an extension of my body. "It takes you twice as long that way," said Beth. "So old-fashioned."

"And you'll be happy to know," said Janet, "the printer's filled with fresh ink."

I headed to the study and began typing. Benny was singing a song in the music room, strumming his guitar. *"Turning and turning in the widening gyre / The falcon cannot hear the falconer."*

Great. No paper in the printer again. I looked around. There by the sofa. What was it doing there? Beside the stack was the course catalogue *The Education Association: Classes for Everyone!* sitting deliberately open to the photo of the head organizer of community classes: Mira. Her wide-set eyes stared back at me.

My stomach tightened as I waited for my poems to print, and it tightened further as that pretty face watched me move through the room before walking out.

Janet will be eyeing me now.

I took my usual seat in the music room and listened as she and Benny finished a silly duet. Her exaggerated voice overpowered his. She sat planted on the arm of his chair watching me. I held her gaze. And when the song ended, I led the applause. I smiled at Benny—only Benny—my flirty smile.

Andy and I sat in a snug inside the Crown Bar. It was located across from the Europa—the most bombed-out hotel during the height of the Troubles—but I felt safe with Andy. The snug's stain-glassed windows and colourful mosaic floors were from the Victorian era. It was like going back in time. Gin Palace. Liquor Saloon. An ornate church of drink.

"First take, Cat. That's all it took."

I had known he'd look good in that blue-and-white-striped shirt the moment I saw it in the trendy Belfast clothing store. The vertical stripes made him look taller, though he didn't need that illusion. He wouldn't accept the gift at first, but I insisted.

"When will it air?"

"Soon," he said, and sipped his Guinness. "We'll watch it together."

I was about to ask *how?* when a white-bearded man appeared at the snug's doorway. "That voice, I knew it. If it isn't the man from Islandmagee in the confession box."

"Tornley. What about ye, mate."

A Northern Irish Hemingway.

"Come, join us," Andy said.

I slid down the wooden bench. Our intimate circle, broken.

Andy told Tornley all about the television taping—was he trying to impress him?—and I realized who he was. Robert Tornley, a writer of stunning short lyrics (so different from Benny's wandering ballads). Small poems with impact that radiated through the page's white space. And here he was, the famous poet, sitting beside me, thanks to Andy. I sipped my pint and listened. I was too tongue-tied to speak.

"All good, all good," Tornley said, smoothing his beard. He sipped from the glass he'd brought in with him. "We're pleased you'll be joining our team at the MacNeice this year. And you, my dear?" he said, turning to me.

"I'm saving her from Benny and Janet," Andy said.

"Ah. You're the one."

Andy chuckled. "Don't scare her."

"Scare her? Why, I have an offer. How about a scholarship to attend the MacNeice? I hate to think of you going all the way back to Canada without some decent instruction."

I stood in the red phone box holding the receiver against my ear, ignoring the dial tone. I used it as a prop to fool cars driving past while I waited for him.

Andy pulled the car to the side of the road and I hopped in. "Duck down," he said.

And I was seven again, hiding below the dashboard in Dad's Buick so Mom wouldn't see me when she came out of the IGA. When Dad tapped my head, out I popped like a jack-in-the-box to surprise her. The joy on Mom's face—

Hiding didn't really bother me. I remained in that cramped position until we hit the dual carriageway.

"Can't wait for you to see Tullymore," Andy said. "My Walden."

"The quarry was mine."

I told Andy how I loved swimming there. The water, mineral-smooth from the limestone, softened the skin. Trilobites and other squiggly-like sea creatures embedded on stone. To touch it was to feel ancient time.

"I know you miss the quarry. At least you had both parents. My da left us when I was a teen."

"Another woman?"

"Cape Town. He got offered a job there, one he couldn't turn down. It was my last year of Grammar School and off we went. I hated the place. They blamed the blacks for everything. Racist pigs. The rugby came in handy then with fights… Mum, she got sick, really sick. They thought it was cancer." He gripped the steering wheel. "You know what it was, Cat? Homesickness. She was homesick for rain and *Coronation Street*, Rathcoole gossip. As soon as she returned for a visit, her symptoms disappeared. She refused to go back. And no way was my da coming home."

The Mourne mountains were coming into view now. We were witnessing the green ease of their rising. I wasn't used to seeing a mountainous landscape. They looked unreal, like the backdrop of a play.

He put his hand on my knee. "It's not easy what's happening to us."

I nodded. His skin's warmth soaked through the denim.

"See that gap up there in the stone wall? That's where they smuggled in goods from the coast. Spices, coffee… carried the contraband on backs of ponies. Hare's Gap."

I know that gap. I—do this.

We got out of the car and began a slow uphill climb through a tunnel of pressing wind. With all the rocks around us, there must be quarries too.

"If we're lucky, we'll see deer."

I stopped.

"Cat?"

The wind burned my tear-filled eyes. Andy saw my pain. He held and sheltered me.

I read through Andy's comments again and tried to ignore the sickening feeling in my stomach. Circles and scratches and suggestions crammed the margins. There wasn't one poem without them. Even "Fire," the poem Benny loved, the last line—*Grief is like waiting for fifty giant black kettles to boil*—had *like* scratched out.

Grief is waiting for fifty giant black kettles to boil.

Simile made into metaphor.

Grief is.

Is it?

I needed to dispel the sickening feeling. Perhaps I was overreacting. Writing was a process, not a destination. I needed to separate the love I had for Andy from his pointed feedback.

When I stepped out of the cottage, Mrs. Petty was heading my way. Her denim skirt fluttered in the breeze. It wasn't "messages" day though she was dressed for it. Perhaps it was a Women's Institute Meeting day.

"There you are," she said. Her hand curled like a hook. "Come in for a cuppa."

I didn't want to come in for a cuppa. I wanted to be alone to absorb what was happening. *I love you, Cat.* He said those words again last night when we talked on the phone. They made me feel airy, a bird in flight. His comments on my poems made me feel grounded, my wings clipped.

Her walk had this urgency to it as I followed her. The sickness inside switched to panic. A phone call from Canada? Was somebody hurt? Sick? Dead? Aunt Doris? Linda? Nana Florence?

Once through the farmhouse door I heard voices in the next room. Stepping closer I saw the feet of two women sitting on the brocade sofa—black leather pumps and nylons, black mules below black ankle-hugging pants.

A jolt travelled through me. It turned into a stake and kept me in place.

Mrs. Petty tugged my arm.

The women turned when I walked in.

"What's this?" I asked.

Mrs. Petty pointed to the wooden chair set directly across the sofa. "Sit," she said. She poured tea into a scarlet cup. The tink of porcelain, of cup meeting plate.

When she handed it to me I was ready to look. Side by side like a pair of oddball friends, they stared at me.

I had no idea they knew one other.

"Now," Mrs. Petty said as if setting the stage. She sat down on the chair beside the sofa.

Ruth set her teacup on the side table. "Caitlin, we understand you've had a hard time in life—losing your parents, being on your own. We understand that."

Was that a smirk? Was she enjoying this?

Janet took hold of Ruth's pause. "And we've seen your progress at the House of Poets. We hope—Benny and I—to see your progress continue."

"Why wouldn't it?"

"People are talking, Caitlin," said Mrs. Petty. "They think I'm running a—" She pulled at her paisley headscarf.

"What she means," said Ruth. "Islandmagee is a tight-knit community. We look out for each other here."

The teacup clattered as I set it down. "Is there anything else?"

"You think you're the first?" blurted Janet.

"What Janet is trying to say, Caitlin, dear—" said Ruth.

I stood. "You think you know. You don't. You don't know a thing. And I'm not your *dear.*"

"Caitlin—"

I would not turn. Out I went into the farmyard, past the fester of clucking chickens, and headed to the red phone box.

I once thought land was water, that's what Aunt Doris had told me before I left for Northern Ireland. We were sitting in her backyard sipping lemonade, watching squirrels run wild along the network of branches. Sparrows, hidden in the hedges, chirped. The chemical blue of the sunken pool sparkled as the pool filter hummed.

Aunt Doris understood why I had to go overseas. She was a homebody but she understood the creative pull. Dad would never approve of my going to a country where people killed one another. But the dead can't stop you from becoming yourself. You can, but the dead can't.

I always felt his presence when I was around her—those long limbs and curved shoulders. She could command a room with her stories just like Dad. They both had that gift. Life is lived forward, but it's retold in story.

"You were just a toddler," she said, "and your parents were so worried about taking you to a restaurant for the first time."

I could feel the eagerness growing on my face. *Keep going.*

"You were no problem at all. That surprised Don and Rusty." She smiled. "What were they expecting? That you'd throw food from the highchair? Sometimes people need a little push. It was a lovely spring day and we went for ice cream afterward and a meander through the park. Strapped in your stroller, you wanted out. So out you went and we watched you toddle off—your arms high like posts. We trailed behind until you stopped at a strip of cement. You wouldn't cross it. You squatted on the grass and stuck out your foot—" She stretched her leg and tapped the patio cement with her open-toe sandal. "Like this."

How strange to have someone tell you something you've done and have no memory of it. "What was I doing?"

"You were being cautious. You thought it wasn't safe. You must've thought it was water—that you might fall, drown even. Some kind of survival instinct. I've never seen a child do that before, be so cautious."

I closed my eyes to the dimming memory and opened the door to the red phone box.

My new bedroom in Carrickfergus was sparse of furniture like the rest of the rented first-floor flat—a pull-out bed Andy had lent me, an easy chair the last renter had left behind. My open suitcase on the bedroom floor served as a drawer. Stacks of books lined the walls. Their coloured spines made me think of my first bedroom—their sporadic brightness like puzzle pieces. Put something down and it stayed there until I chose to play with it again. Immersing myself in imaginary worlds, I made animals and dolls talk and move and travel on journeys—over waterfalls (the bathroom sink) and cliffs (the bed). My toys didn't fight and they never killed. No guns or bows and arrows. For some reason they were always on the run—*they're coming, they're coming*—unable to settle in the furniture of their jungled world.

The red-door cottage sat empty now. The white walls were bare again. But the Scotch tape I'd used to tack up pictures and postcards from home had ripped the paint off upon removal. In that way, I guess, I left my mark.

The rent for the flat wasn't cheap. I had to tap into more savings. Investments from my inheritance, from selling the quarry. As painful as that was, only ghosts remained. Aunt Doris set me up with a financial advisor. For the past year or so, monthly statements had showed the numbers going up. This wasn't happening now. But it was worth it to be close enough to Andy and away from gathering gossip.

My new flat's near a castle. What I told Aunt Doris, Linda, and Nana Florence in my letters home. Not: *I'm in love.* I had nobody to say that to.

I was alone a lot now—able to run and eat when I wanted, sleep when I wanted, write. A poet's dream. So why did I feel so lonely? He came by most days. And days he couldn't, he phoned. During those conversations I imagined him in his second-floor study looking out at that sliver of sea. Once we hung up I imagined him falling asleep on the study's single bed while below Mira slept with Chel in the master bedroom.

I stared at the notebook on my lap. The silence was a presence of distraction. Nothing reverberated. No crackling fire. Not even the annoyance of Mrs. Petty.

"That's enough," I said, dropping the notebook on the pullout bed. I walked down the hallway into the living room to face the emptiness head on. I started flapping my arms like a determined bird about to take flight, a land-locked bird that needed water to kick-start her departure, and as I circled the square, my walk turned into a run. "Enough! Enough!" I chanted, breathing harder each time, until the sound lost all meaning.

I was tired when I stopped. Sweat trickled down my back and between my breasts. I put my hand on my chest to feel something beating, wanting out.

A half hour later, I carried my dirty laundry into town to the local laundromat. I read MacNeice while waiting for the wash cycle to complete. A mechanical dryer did the work of the seaside wind and Portmuck sun. I folded the load and carried it back to the flat, thankful another day had ended.

"I don't believe this," I said the next day when Andy finally arrived at the flat. I'd been waiting for more than two hours. (What if something had happened to him? Who would I ask?) There was no time for that now. I grabbed hold of what I'd received in the mail.

"Here," I said, handing him the letter. I took a deep breath. "I'm going to fail."

Andy paced the living room as he read, his stride deliberate, like his thinking.

"We'll see about this," he said.

I knew he would help me. My mind returned to my father. "They gave you a B in art?" he'd said, waving my report card. "This should be an A. You're always an A." The very next day, unbeknownst to me, he spoke to Mrs. Lennox, the art teacher. "It's done," he said that night when he called me into his study. He tapped the report card on his desk and smiled. When I looked down I saw an A above a scratched-out B, and above the floating A, Mrs. Lennox's initials in dark red ink.

"Bollocks," said Andy, his eyes tightened. "They already gave you permission. They're trying to get at me through you. That's what this is. I'm sorry, Cat."

Weren't they trying to get at me through me?

Andy looked around the living room as if seeing the emptiness for the first time. We always went straight to the bedroom. "Crikey, there's nowhere to sit. Let's go to the kitchen."

We sat in folded chairs and sipped the Guinness I'd poured into pint glasses stolen from a nearby pub—it was so easy to slip them into my knapsack.

"They're trying to scare you, Cat."

"What if they tell Mira about us?"

"Mira knows about us. You're my friend. She knows that."

"Come on, Andy. Friend?"

"Look. We need time. We have time now, thanks to this place. You gotta let me figure this out. It's all about the timing."

Timing. Time. *Tempus fugit*. Time's winged chariot won't wait. Someone said that recently. Why couldn't I remember who it was?

"You have to trust what's happening here." He slid his chair next to mine and lifted my chin.

"No," I said, and picked up my memoir, the hodgepodge of prose. "This is a mess."

Living outside a routine—no runs, little sleep, plus the drinking and now the little brown pipe Andy brought each visit which led to late-night munchies—ketchup crisps, Jammy Dodgers, cheese toasties—I was out of balance, lethargic, fat.

Andy flicked through the memoir. "I know what this needs," he said, standing up. His brown brogues clicked against the worn linoleum as he continued to shuffle through the pages. He tossed me the pen from his shirt pocket and pushed my spiral notebook towards me.

He cleared his throat. "Listen."

I did—to his fast-moving words and I wrote them down. I wrote down what he said like a secretary, and before my eyes grew a chain of prose, page after page, until my memoir was done.

They say it's about meeting the one. Your soulmate. Love of your life. I grew up with that romantic notion, with dreams and visions of being rescued. One had me abandoned with a flat tire on a dark country road. Cold and alone, I stand helpless, waiting, until headlights bloom from the distance. The driver pulls over and out pops Robert Redford, the strawberry-blond actor my mother loved. I can't believe it's him. He guides me to his cherry-red convertible and off we go to his castle. He falls in love with me. Sometimes we kiss. Sometimes we do more than kiss. Thankfully, it's a recurring dream.

I never thought about the consequence of my helpless state. A flat tire is easy to fix if you have the tools (which I did).

I thought he would help me with the memoir, not write it. I thought he would show me, not tell. Writing his words down verbatim, I saw how it was done. Too late. My M.A. thesis was typed, bound, and heading to the House of Poets in a black taxi. I refused to go back there to deliver it. I saw them the way Andy saw them—King and Queen of Ego Castle. A couple so full of themselves, they'd lost touch with reality.

"The look on their faces when the cabbie arrives at their front door." Andy passed me the little brown pipe.

I inhaled and passed it back. The weedy smoke clotted my throat. "They'll hate that dedication." I tried not to cough.

"I didn't expect that." He smiled.

"I know," I said, remembering his reaction.

We were safe now. There was nothing they could do. The external examiner Andy talked to on the phone the other week didn't have an issue with my memoir. There'd never been an issue. It was all a ruse. Even so, Andy placed a caveat in my thesis: *Special permission was given to substitute an academic paper with memoir.*

I no longer had a fireplace. Only candles. Flames multiplied through the glass darkly as I sat on the windowsill waiting for him. Each time a car turned down the dead-end road and I saw approaching headlights, my heart raced to meet the moment. But the driver either parked by the water or made a U-y and drove away. I was near the sea but couldn't hear it. The Lough tamed incoming waves. I missed the sea's music.

I didn't dare look at the reflection staring back at me. That pale, adulterous face, primped-up sweetly clean, waiting for hands to strip her body naked.

I was free from prying eyes—yes—but nobody knew me here. He could see I was lonely. He could sense such things. *Stay a little longer, Andy, please.* I hated sounding desperate.

Last night while he dressed, I lifted his tucked-in shirt to kiss his soft hairy belly.

"Stop." He nudged me away. "It's hard enough leaving you."

"You're sure about Saturday?" I asked again.

"If I wasn't, I'd tell you."

"But Mrs. Petty and Ruth, Janet—"

"The three witches? They haven't said anything to Mira. Besides, Mira knows I'd never leave Grace with someone irresponsible. The way Grace talks about you—you made quite an impression that day. She's dying to see Canada now. It's all she talks about."

Mira was heading to Donegal with Chel to visit her cousin. Grace had a sleepover and wanted to stay in Islandmagee. Andy had a reading at a library in Belfast Saturday morning. *Would you mind helping out, Cat?*

When he left, I lay on his side of the pullout bed—what

once was my side—to smell his scent. Closing my eyes, I touched myself to sleep.

I opened the flat's front door and she came running towards me, her arms circling my waist. "You're my new buddy," she said, looking up. The citrus scent from her curls was the same as his: the family shampoo.

"I am, am I?" She saw me as a teacher, as someone to admire.

He was standing by his car. The wind ruffled the sleeves of his denim jacket but not his hair. Whenever I tried to run my hands through it, he guarded it like a shield.

Don't touch.

The craving to touch.

"She's all yours," he said and waved goodbye.

From the living-room window we watched him drive away. The room was saturated with morning light, a yellow glisten.

"Dead-on!" said Grace, circling the emptiness. Her trainers (not sneakers) echoed through the space. "It's like a dance floor." She did a shimmy and a cartwheel.

We were twins that day without even trying. Blue jeans and pink sweaters. Our curls, loose. When we stepped outside and headed towards the roadway that led to the Norman castle, she took my hand.

We passed a garden, tangled with weeds. "Cat! Your favourite plant."

"Nice try," I said, curling my fingers.

She giggled.

Weeks ago, before my move to Carrickfergus, I hadn't heard her calling out my name. My Walkman blocked her voice. Not until she caught up with me, carrying a loaf of bread (Veda, his favourite), her purchase from the corner store, did I see her. When we stopped by the roadside to chat, I nervously bent to pluck a leaf in the ditch.

"Ouch!" I said, pulling back.

"That's a nettle you touched."

I looked at the culprit, the coarsely toothed leaves. Stinging nettle. Yes, I'd been warned—by Mrs. Petty, by Janet. *Watch your legs on those runs.*

Too late. The sting was in me.

Grace yanked a fistful from another plant and scrunched it in her hands. "The good green," she said, passing it to me. "Dock in, nettle out."

Cool like aloe vera or pink calamine lotion on itchy chickenpox spots, my mother's caring hands over my pockmarked back, sponging the pain with a damp terry cloth, the dock leaves soothed the burning sensation.

"The look on your face that day," said Grace. "Soooo funny."

I made an attempt at recapturing that face, the painful shock.

She laughed into a high-pitched giggle.

The Norman castle stood in full view now. "Have you been here before?" I asked.

"Mr. Pick took us."

"This year?"

"No. He taught me last year, too. But I won't have him next year."

Next year. How it sat like the slippery edge of a waking dream. My negotiations with the school board were brief but fruitful. I could extend my leave but would have to replace a teacher mid-year in another school, one I might not like. The risk was worth it to have more time with Andy.

Grace squeezed my hand. "Race ya!"

We ran up the drawbridge into the castle. I told Grace we didn't have castles back home. The closest I could think of was a fort. Fort Niagara. Fort York. Fort Erie. The War of 1812.

Barracks, pits, and fortified walls with slots for cannons to blast the enemy.

"Look what they did to the baddies," said Grace after I purchased our tickets.

The castle floor opened to below, to a hole big enough for a bucket of hot tar to land on invaders' heads. The Murder Hole. Grace continued to look down. I turned away.

A castle prepared for invasion. From foreigners who wanted to take.

I peered through the wall—a slit of cold stone—and saw to the other side. County Down. Home of the Mourne Mountains. Andy's Walden.

I couldn't stop thinking of him.

I hadn't planned on taking. We don't plan to take.

Was that how Dad rationalized his relationship with Linda? Yet Dad had someone to be true to. *Rusty, always my champion.* The words on Mom's ID bracelet after she lost a close tennis match, now my bracelet thanks to Dad.

Who was I betrothed to?

After visiting the banquet hall, the keep, the inner courtyard, the ramparts, the gatehouse and chapel, we headed back outside and wandered through the narrow winding streets that had carried routes from medieval days and found a café.

"Mmm," I said, eyeing a plate. "Those fries look good."

"Chips, Cat!" said Grace. "Not *fries*." She grabbed hold of the plastic bottle beside the vase of yellow flowers. "And this is *red sauce,* not ketchup." She smiled. "What are you like?"

I'd heard that expression many times now. *What are you like?* A question that didn't require an answer.

What was I like?

"You and your little sister," said the waitress, directly at me. "Ready to order?" One hand was on her hip like an act of impatience, but her eyes were warm.

"Chips, pleeease," Grace said, winking at me. "Right, Sis?"

I was alone again but I had my own room. Andy had a single room too, but on a higher floor where the real writers stayed. His car was in the lot—I saw it parked there when I made my way into the main building for room assignment, so I knew he was here. So were others—writers, intellectuals, strangers.

The MacNeice Festival took place on the grounds of an old private school nestled by the edge of the Antrim coast. The grounds were green and lively and the buildings brick and golden. But the view to the water was blocked by walls.

In the breeze I could smell the sea's churning.

Unlike the House of Poets, there were no workshops here. Lectures and talks engaged the mind, the intellect—*The Effects of Isolation on 19th Century Verse; The Spirituality of Planter Poets*—topics I didn't care about. But I looked forward to Andy's poetry presentation on Islandmagee.

"The Canadian's here."

"Thank you, Mr. Tornley. Thank you so much for this."

"My pleasure," said Tornley. "I'm anxious to hear what you think. I'd like you to meet one of the founders, Colleen McPherson."

I extended my hand to the tall woman standing beside him. She tilted her head like a watchful bird. "I do hope you enjoy your time here." She smiled. "Lots to do!" And she left us standing there.

"She's part of the official ceremonies," said Tornley, checking his watch. "Any minute now. And yer man, is he here?"

Yer man. I wasn't fooled by that now. "I haven't seen him yet."

"Ah, speak of the devil," said Tornley, looking sideways.

Andy slapped the famous poet on the back. "What about ye, Torn." He looked my way. "Cat."

I smiled.

"Cat?" said Tornley.

At that moment a blast of trumpets sounded through the auditorium. We stepped inside and watched a parade of men march in a line. The two leading the parade carried a banner with the image of Louis MacNeice on it—high cheekbones and chiselled jaw, he resembled a film star. It was the kind of banner Orangemen used during the Twelfth of July parades. I'd seen pictures in newspapers and footage on TV—gold fringes and over-the-top colours, King Billy on his rampant white horse, red hand of Ulster. Tribal images that signalled: *no surrender.*

Despite the camaraderie at the MacNeice—over breakfast and morning lectures, lunch and afternoon lectures, dinners and readings—I found myself missing the music room, looking out at the sea and Muck Island, yearning for Andy. Though Andy was here.

His face was full of energy; his mouth raced with talk and jokes and anecdotes. Everyone knew him and he knew everyone. He had no time for me.

I had known this would happen. My mind knew. My "intellect." But my heart ached for otherwise.

"We can't let on," he whispered. "You know that." We were heading to the dining hall for the evening meal.

We didn't sit side by side along the long wooden table like I hoped, but across and one over, kitty corner.

A new woman arrived and squeezed herself next to Andy. She had an accent, one I didn't recognize. Eastern European? Maybe. Her eyes were arctic blue. No, more like antifreeze. She introduced herself to Andy, only Andy. I was forced to watch. Her blonde hair was glacial and her cheekbones cut like rock, like a high-paid model. She was touching him, tapping his strong forearm, her manicured fingertips landing there lightly. She edged in, close enough to brush his knees and let her miniskirted legs slide casually against him.

He made it easy for her to continue—talking, laughing, saying things I couldn't hear.

"I'm not feeling well," I said, standing up, stepping back from the never-ending table.

There was nothing to do in my dorm room and I couldn't sit down, so I paced back and forth to stop the agitation needling inside me. I thought of Mom's pincushions. Then voodoo dolls. Andy was certain Janet used them. "She's a white witch from Salem, not Boston like she claims. Each time I feel a sting, I'm sure it's her." Or was he joking? Andy detested all things having to do with the occult or black magic. I'd long since hidden my tarot cards from him. If they hadn't been a gift from Linda, a concrete reminder of home, I would've thrown them out. Pinocchio by a fire. Was that the last one I pulled from the pack? Or was I mixing up images? Did it even matter?

Another door opening and closing down the hallway, another resident preparing for evening readings, a soft knock. "Cat?"

I couldn't leave him standing there. I opened the door. He came in and closed it.

"What the hell happened back there?"

"Nothing happened." I cradled my stomach.

"Something you ate, you think?"

"How could it be something I ate if I didn't eat anything?"

"What are you doing?"

"What do you mean, what am I doing?"

He looked at my shuffling feet. My cage had closed in.

"Moving helps," I said.

"So that's it, cramps." He kissed me on the forehead like a child. "You had me worried. I'll see you at the reading."

"I don't know," I said. I couldn't think.

"Cramps," he said, and turned to leave.

It was my mother who told me to move whenever cramps came. "Get up and move, dear," she said in her soft nursing voice whenever she saw me in discomfort.

Sometimes I didn't want to move. Sometimes I just wanted to sit in my teenage nest of hurt on the edge of the chesterfield and be a big egg of pain.

The morning light penetrated the gauzy curtain. I checked my watch. Andy's talk on Islandmagee was starting soon.

She was there when I walked in, but I was ready for her this time. I sat in a row near the front so I wouldn't have to look at her. He nodded my way as he took centre stage. I nodded back. Our exchange like our secret telephone signal: *ring once, hang up, count to ten, ring again.*

The beginning of the last day of the MacNeice. Nothing could be as painful as last night—the sight of her naked body entwined with his weaving through my dreams.

"Don't be shy," Andy said to those entering the auditorium. I turned. Women mostly. Was that right? I looked again. It was.

If I'd been another kind of woman, I would've felt proud being the chosen. I had his skin, his moans. But who knew? He seemed fresh game for the taking.

Andy shared his poems about Islandmagee and the stories behind them. He wowed them with his deep voice and roguish charm. He fed off their smiles and eyelash flutters.

She went up to him afterwards. I saw her shapely outline in my peripheral vision under that sharp crop of blonde hair. There she goes again touching his forearm, below the sleeve of his black T-shirt.

"Nice work, yer man," said Tornley.

I turned from where I was standing, to the freshly deserted row behind me. "Yes," I said.

Tornley smiled, his lips hidden by his bushy beard. Andy's beard, trim and tight, highlighted his mouth, his full lips.

"That Islandmagee's quite the place," Tornley said. "If Andy's poems weren't so bloody good, I'd be tempted to write about it myself. How's your writing coming along?"

"It's coming." It wasn't.

"You're living on here, so I've heard."

"By the castle in Carrick."

"That's on my way. I'll give you a lift."

"Oh," I said, feeling queasy. "I should take the bus."

"Nonsense," he said, waving his hand. "You keep good company. Two o'clock good?"

We were heading to the dining hall for lunch when Andy spoke loudly in my ear. "You know I have a car."

"You never said—"

"You playing with me?"

"What do you mean?"

"He fancies you."

"Who?"

"Tornley."

"He does not."

"I've seen the way he looks at you."

"When?"

"All the time. Since that night at The Crown. And don't tell me you don't warm to him."

"What's that supposed to mean?"

Grabbing my wrist, he guided me to a wall, away from sight. His brogues had nothing to click on, the slush of our soles across grass.

I looked up and saw a patch of blue beyond greying clouds. I wanted to disappear into that patch but I knew I had to go through this. "He's too old for me, Andy."

"Right. And your professor wasn't?"

"Dr. Delio? Why are you bringing him up?"

"You have a little pattern going, don't you think?"

I'd told Andy about my married thesis professor, our complicated attachment. We were in Dublin when he had asked about my past, a tipsy conversation over pints. I thought it was safe.

"What am I supposed to do?" I said, and stopped walking to demand an answer, but when I looked behind all I saw was his black T-shirt growing smaller and smaller.

"You know," said Tornley. He flicked on the windshield wipers. "I used to be good friends with Benny, back in the day."

The wipers smeared the mist. "I know," I said.

He tapped the steering wheel and glanced out at the foggy sea. The Antrim Coast had a view that rivalled California's.

"Pity the weather. You're missing the view. The rope bridge, have you been there?"

"Carrick-a-Rede?" Suspended high in the air—the vulnerable bridge—the long drop below—it was a well-known tourist attraction, like the Giant's Causeway. I knew it through seeing postcards.

"It connects mainland to a wee island. Fisherman used it to get across for hundreds of years. A popular tourist attraction now. Not as tacky as some."

"*Carrick* means 'rock,' right?"

"Rock in the road. The trick is to not look down, to keep your eyes forward like a tightrope walker."

"Especially if you're afraid of heights." I thought of that summer day Mom and I went to Crystal Beach Amusement Park. I'd begged her to take me on the Ferris wheel. When the ride came to a stop, we swung back and forth in the open-air cage. I loved the commanding view. But Mom closed her eyes and made sharp intakes with her breath. It was then I realized she'd faced her fear for me.

"Get Andy to take you," he said, and rolled the window down a crack.

I inhaled. "The smell of green."

"The smell of home," said Tornley, looking my way. "Tell me, what was it *really* like at the House of Poets?"

"Well," I said, remembering Andy's words. "They drink too much, way too much, and they're disorganized... Last fall they kept telling us these famous poets were coming from America to give readings and workshops." I shook my head. "They never came. Andy calls it Ego Castle."

He laughed. "He's not far off. Thinks he's the best, Benny. Always did. Janet's devotion feeds that. A shame, envy." He coughed, hesitated, and turned to me. "I've had my bad times too," he said, as if he knew something.

"Part of the territory, isn't it? For poets."

"You would know, Caitlin."

The wipers grew louder in my head. Tornley knows. Of course he knows.

"You write about yours."

"Oh," I said with relief.

"I'm much older than you, but the loss is the same."

"Yes. Loss is loss."

He smiled. "And love is love."

The mist fattened to raindrops. Little pings.

"They live on in your poems though. Strange how that happens, the artist's resurrection."

"Yes. I thought it would hurt writing about them. It doesn't."

"It's not therapy what we do, what people think we do. It's the work of the spirit, the soul. How could that hurt? The hurt is in not doing it."

After waving goodbye to Tornley, I locked the door to the flat. He honked twice as he drove away. I waved from the window. I could no longer ignore the ache in the coil of my stomach.

I looked at the phone, lifeless on its cradle. I didn't have an answering machine. Only Andy had my number. I picked up the receiver to see if it was working. It was. I slammed it back down.

Run. Go on.

What if he calls?

Let him call. You've done nothing wrong. What have you done wrong?

I sat on the windowsill and watched the light seed to dark. I was inside the husk now.

I was getting good at waiting, at parcelling off tender pieces of myself.

That night I awoke with a horrible premonition. He's with her, that's why he never called.

I don't care if Mira answers or if the ringing wakes up the girls.

He answered on the third ring.

"You're there."

"Cat?" His voice was groggy.

"You're not with her."

"Her?"

"The European. The—"

"You mean Elena?"

"Is that her name?"

"Cat, I tried calling you."

"You did? When?" Was I running the bath then?

"Did you think I wouldn't?"

"Tornley invited me to a reading next week. I said no. I told him no."

"We need to protect what we have. You understand that now. I'm glad." He sighed. "I wish I was there, holding you. But let's get some sleep now, okay?"

"Tomorrow?"

"Tomorrow. Night, Cat."

World is suddener than we fancy it. MacNeice's line came back to me as I snuggled under the bedcovers and closed my eyes to imagine the muscling sea, the strings of rain pummelling the stone-grey water from our view at Brown's Bay.

I wasn't alone when I was with him.

I stood up from the kitchen table and extended my arms and legs like John Cleese in a Monty Python skit. I was determined to keep a straight face despite Andy's bursts of laughter as I walked across the worn linoleum doing my polished imitation, but it wasn't easy.

"That's it! That's Benny," he said, slapping his knee. "Do the Janet now," he said, exhaling from the little brown pipe.

Hands tucked at my sides, I puffed out my cheeks and shuffled forward with a tipsy glaze in my eyes. He laughed even harder.

I bit my tongue to stifle the giggling.

"Pickled," he said after another inhale. "From all that gin. *Oh, the kittiwakes, oh, the seals, let me tell you...*"

Our stomachs were sore from the late-night laughter and from gorging on the overpriced biscuits and crisps I'd purchased earlier that day at the garage (not gas station). We laughed so hard the tears kept coming.

Later, our bodies wrapped around each other, our naked sated bodies, I rested my head in the crook of his neck, the scent of musk and lemon. I whimpered and licked the tip of his ear. "Puppies in the litter," I said playfully.

"Pet," he said, patting my head.

I never thought of myself as gullible. *Still waters run deep.* That was how I saw myself. A water of stillness like the quarry on windless days. People underestimate the quiet. They think you're naive, dumb, mute. That you don't pick up on things or have a voice within you. But I know from experience how strong quiet is. The internal world—always talking. To you. At you. With feelings and images. The shape the mind gives to a passing cloud, how it turns it to a face or animal, and those energy vibrations from strangers—hostile, sizzling coils. Hear the tension in their voices, and your feelings are confirmed, your intuition to stay away. It never occurred to me that Tornley might fancy me. My feelings didn't connect to how Andy saw things. But I wanted to make Andy happy, the way I wanted to make Dad happy and find my peace within.

I thought back to the boy who bullied me in grade school, his hazel eyes like evil slits. He'd stare and chant, "Cat got your tongue?" and my face would burn from the chill of his staring, proof I was in his trap. Thankfully, he soon got bored with me standing animal stiff—a deer or rabbit—and off he'd go.

I'd been born with stillness, an internal escape. My mother had it—I see that now—a silence to slip into.

The Christmas after we went to New York City, the second Christmas without her, we stayed home at the quarry. We didn't bother getting a tree even though we still had all the ornaments Mom had painstakingly made—red felt bows and glittery fruit bouquets, bagged and tied and boxed in the back hall closet. Why bother? The days would pass and we'd have to take them down again.

Usually Dad asked what I wanted for Christmas.

"For you," he said, smiling like a kid.

The box was heavy, so the gift had weight. I set it on my lap. Snow hit the family room window in spastic chunks though the sky was clear. The sporadic wind was whipping it off the nearby cedar branches. He was sitting where Mom used to sit, watching me.

"Oh," I said and touched the animal softness.

He leaned forward. "Hold it up. Go on."

The coat was so long, even when I stretched out my arms I was too close to see it.

"Give it here," he said, grabbing hold. He guided me into the maroon-satin lining.

It fit. I could feel the fit. But I still couldn't see it.

"Come on," he said.

I followed him down the hallway into the master bedroom. Mom's hospital bed was long gone, just the king-size bed now, but the smell of decay ghosted through the wall's cedar knots. I could always smell it.

I looked in Mom's mirror and saw my head above a furry body, an animal I didn't know the name of.

"You don't like it," he said, his voice flat, deflated. He yanked it off me and left the room.

I stood like an abandoned mannequin.

I wanted to tell him—*It's not what people my age wear. I'll be a freak.*

"Ungrateful," I heard him mutter down the hall.

It wasn't until the second death—Dad's—that I was told I was brave. "To go through this again," said a family friend during Dad's visitation.

"She's coping so well," others whispered.

Was I? My core held the hollow of a mummified mouse.

Despite the black pit, grief—loss—tossed you onto an unwanted platform. There I was, front and centre on the small-town stage.

Coping well can be a ruse. That deep-water stillness misinterpreted, pits with unending depths and an endless supply of passive resources. Get through the grief and do and be anything. There had to be a reason for loving a married man.

Love wires the body to a new fuse. He—the source—rewires you to his house. This wild unnerving, coupled with an at-ease attachment must mean—he's the one, the only one you'll do anything for to prove your body right.

III

My old apartment wasn't big enough for both of us. We needed a two-bedroom—one for sleeping, the other for Andy to write in, and a location away from Burlington where Aunt Doris lived, with enough distance from the elementary school I was contracted to teach at. The second room would give Andy the space needed during our short time in Canada. He already had drafts for his efforts, plus hopeful scraps in the notebook he kept tucked in his back pocket.

Mira had agreed to his sabbatical, though not at first. When she came across one of my love letters inside one of his poetry books (I never did find out which one. Maybe the Carver, beside "Late Fragment"?) she shook the evidence in his face—he was sitting at the kitchen table, eating his late-night supper, beans on toast—and what did he say? "You're snooping in *my* things?" In no time at all he had her on the defensive.

He told her he thought I was in love in him, that he felt sorry for me. He'd become attached to me, yes, but it definitely wasn't love.

"What's that supposed to mean?" I asked when he came by the flat that evening. His knee shook under the kitchen table. I could feel the vibrations in my bones, the pressing tremble.

"I had to tell her something. You know better than anyone how complicated this is."

"You mean Dad and Linda?"

He nodded.

"Dad loved Mom. He always loved Mom."

"Like I love you."

She didn't ask about sex so he didn't have to lie about that. Some wives don't want to know.

They'd reached an icy compromise. Yes, he could go to Canada for six months, but she wanted financial support in his absence. Then they would see how things stood.

He said what he needed to say to make her understand. Our world—the literary world—wasn't the world she lived in. Literary couples weren't normal couples. Any literary biography would tell you that.

This was her strategy—for him to go away to know if she still wanted him. That's what I read in the cavern of space between the few words he said about her, their situation, and how she'd been handled by him. To ask for details was to get him going. To ask him questions was to reveal a lack of belief. To let him be was to show him my belief in him, something Mira could no longer do. It was what I had over her.

"We knew this would happen, didn't we," I said.

"Loss brought you to me," Andy said, that last night in the flat. "Think about it—your parents. How else would we have met?"

"I feel them sometimes."

He looked up at the ceiling, at the candle's shadowy flickers, their wavering dance. "I feel them in you, too."

I could finish my teaching obligations with the school board, and then we'd fall into our future together. Mira was sure to grant him a divorce. She just needed time and space. What a relief Andy lived in the North. I thought back to Niamh's comment: *No divorce in Ireland.*

He passed me the little brown pipe. He could see I wanted it. He watched me inhale. He knew how much money I had now, my inheritance.

We had no secrets.

I barely got through the day being "Ms. Maharg." The class I'd been assigned to—grade six—was one I'd never taught before. I was used to teaching younger grades. Surly with attitude, these thirty-one prepubescent students, no sweetness left in their simmering hormones. They called my black ankle boots "witch's boots." Go ahead, call me witch. I had the man I loved. What else mattered?

Andy couldn't believe the biting snow-winds, black ice, and frigid temperatures. Despite his muscular bulk he wasn't equipped for our winter, so I bought him a down-filled jacket and heavy gloves. Now *he* was the one learning new words: *toque, toboggan, Tim Hortons.* But his ears didn't ache from the sound of our mild-mannered accents, only the bone-numbing cold.

"Malls and more malls," Andy said, eyeing the road. We were driving for groceries—it was too cold to walk. He turned into the parking lot, one hand on the wheel. He had no trouble driving on the other side; the challenge was easy. "Where's the culture," he said, pulling up his black hood before opening the car door. "Your culture is weather."

True to his alpha nature, he located the nearest pub—The Shaw—an Irish writer who didn't inspire him. "Too poncy," he said after sipping his first pint, his top lip curling to the gumline. He looked at his Guinness. "Too flat."

We'd just finished mailing another money order to Mira. My money. But I said it was his too, which was why I gave him cash, so our daily spending wouldn't seem so one-sided. It was the right thing to do. It was. He'd sacrificed everything to be with me, and despite many drafts he still had poems to write. He'd secured a new publisher, an innovative press Tornley had recently published with. They were counting on Andy to help grow their reputation.

After another long day at school, another long week, I came back to the apartment and found him on top of the unmade futon still wearing his nightclothes—maroon T-shirt and briefs—a biography of Beckett beside him. The look on Andy's face was like the words on the cover: *I can't go on.* Turned to this place, this emotional plane, he was the epitome of grief, the grief of my past, my quarry. I thought back to the Yeats painting, the bull's-eye black that herded the eye. And yet above that black floated the horse of white hope.

I sat on the edge of the mattress and cupped his knee. "What can I do? What can I do to help?"

"Bring Grace over. Chel's too young, but Grace can do it. Mid-term break's coming up."

"What about Mira?"

"Haven't I said we'll be together? Haven't we always been together, Cat?"

My cold hand warmed from his skin. I moved it higher, along his upper thigh. His muscles still held the years of rugby in them. Tilting back on the pillow, he guided me. I fondled the cushion plum cold and taking hold, I found the right rhythm. He didn't take long. My yes to Grace released him.

We got into a pattern after that, a daily countdown. Letters arrived from overseas with *SWAK* crayoned on the back. *Can't wait to see you!* Our adulterous guilt, what we didn't talk about, lay dormant like the sap in winter trees and buried bulbs in frozen gardens.

Daily perks helped push me through the boring institutional routine. Lunchtime phone calls to Andy helped divide the long tiring day, as did the noon drive to Tim Hortons.

I did everything possible to avoid the staffroom. What did I have to say to middle-aged people with middle-class lives?

I'm sure they talked about me. My deliberate absence—a dare, a threat. *Who do you think you are?* But payday would have its perks now. My master's diploma had arrived in the mail. Another degree would make my salary go up.

"See?" Andy said. "Told you it was a bluff."

But had the words been mine? I didn't want to think about it.

Another degree behind my name. No time to be a poet.

I was sitting on a strip-mall bench outside the laundromat, enjoying the March sun. I closed my eyes to take in the warmth. Andy was inside exchanging loonies for quarters for the dryer when I heard a voice call my name from the parking lot. When I opened my eyes, I saw Andy inside those familiar bearded features. It was Dr. Delio.

"Caitlin, you're back… you never returned my—I wrote you when you were overseas, didn't you get my letters?"

Andy stood at the doorway, eyeing the man eyeing me. Had he heard my professor's question?

"You need something, mate?"

"Andy," I said, walking over to him.

"Well, would you look at that," he said, glaring past my shoulders.

When I turned, Dr. Delio was nowhere to be seen.

"Didn't even bring his dry-cleaning in. Ran like a scared rabbit when he saw me."

I peered into the parking lot.

"You want to chase after your old lover, is that it?" He paused. "Letters. You never mentioned letters."

He slammed the apartment door and dropped the basket with a thud. He'd yanked out the clothes the moment the dryer had stopped spinning. I wanted to fold them to prevent them from wrinkling but didn't dare touch the heap.

He paced the living room floor. "You'd met me by then. That's why you won't tell me. You had to write that wanker first for him to write back. When are you going to admit that?"

"It was before Dublin, okay? And he wasn't my lover. He was never my lover."

"Right," he said, dismissing my words with his hand. "Before Dublin... before Brown's Bay?"

I folded my arms.

He stopped pacing. "After all I've done."

"There was nothing in my letter. I only wrote the once. What does it matter? I never got his replies."

"Not one? You expect me to believe that?" He leaned against the wall by the front window.

I walked towards the bedroom.

"Go ahead, then," he said. "Get some sleep."

"Can't we forget this?"

"He'll be sniffing around, you watch."

The light through the window gave a powdery glow, and I saw a boy standing there, a Rathcoole boy, wanting to be held.

"Andy, I never lied to you. It's you I love."

He let out a long floating scarf of a sigh, a release that wrapped around my neck and wound tightly around me.

Statistics show the husband rarely leaves the wife for the other woman, but I knew I wasn't a statistic. Our bond held amazing strength. The memory of that commercial came back to me: the man with the hard hat Krazy-Glued to a steel girder, holding on to the rim of his hat, his long legs wild and flying.

We were sitting in Tim Hortons eating doughnuts. Grace tongued the powdery sweetness. Andy swallowed the last of his Boston Cream.

Grace loved Canada. She didn't miss her mother, not in a homesick way. She shone under our attention and made us giggle again, and though she loved her little sister, she was happy to be away from Chel. Her *I-want* cries and fist-thumping tantrums had increased, so she told us. We didn't want to think why.

"So, how is your mother?" Andy finally asked.

"She's painting the house, room by room," Grace said. "She's moved all the furniture. We watch the telly looking the other way."

I took a deep breath and finished my double chocolate.

His mood could go either way now—he could view Mira's behaviour as *I'm getting on without you* or as a middle-finger threat to his domain. She was clearing her past, a sign that made me feel safer.

I thought of the game Monopoly. To own the most properties was to experience the thrill of bankrupting your opponents. Their wads of cash became your wads of cash. Yet even in your newfound power, you're open to chance, to the change that comes with the flip of a card, and off you go to jail.

Reveal your get-out-of-jail card and you're free from the chains of chance. I looked at Grace eating her doughnut, licking the centre to savour the cream. She smiled back at me, her blue eyes warm. My sweet get-out-of-jail card, there, that girl.

The streets looked smaller than I remembered, but the Escarpment hovered behind Grimsby (where we lived before the quarry) like it had during my early childhood. Evergreens and maples lined the shouldering rise. Grace didn't see what I saw—a pigtailed girl sitting in the front seat of the Malibu with her father, helping him with Saturday errands while her mother slept in the king-size bed after another late night of nursing in ICU. They were on their way to the IGA, the place the little girl called *Igga*. See her skip through the store to the cereal aisle, her mouth watering like the milk she'll pour over her bowl of choice, the cartoon faces singing their siren songs: *They're GRRREAT! They're magically delicious! Can't get enough of that Sugar Crisp!* Too many stations cramming her head, and the Technicolor wobbly and fuzzy. In her mind now, Count Chocula's fangs drip with blood and Frankenberry's face is puckered with warts.

I shook away the images that came when I couldn't find my father as I ran down the never-ending cereal aisle.

Grace didn't understand why I called it the Upside-Down House. "Why, Cat?" We were halfway up Kingsway Crescent, my old home in full view.

"Bedrooms downstairs, kitchen and family room, up."

"That's it?"

"Most houses are designed the other way."

"Like ours," she said.

Andy stopped the car at the end of the long driveway. The hedge I was told never to go past was no longer there. That physical barrier gone, along with the screened-in porch—it was walled in with glass. A house with new history and an ugly wagon wheel nailed to the front to prove it. I didn't want to think about changes inside.

The hedge wasn't the only thing ripped away. I thought of the pineapple-like stub in the bloom's centre, the spikes inside the pale pink-white cup. I loved to peel the petal's outer layer to find the cooling gel before it shrivelled to rust on the driveway. Every year I'd wait for the blooms to open, and when they peaked with full fleshy beauty they appeared permanent. But the opening led to falling—

Gone.

I was glad I was in the backseat, the privacy like a gift. Clenching my hands, I sat aching with nostalgia until the hedge returned and the magnolia tree was there in full bloom, that cumbersome wagon-wheel pitched and burned.

The Horseshoe Falls were tricky to see through the rising mist. We listened to the sound of blue fury and watched the water fall in white threads and blue chunks. *Niagarously roaring.* The true Niagara. We leaned over the stone wall, the only guard rail. No drowning woman here to save, only the vertigo pull to jump.

I looked at Andy, his face moist from the mist. I could tell what he was thinking. We often thought the same thing at the same time.

"You think she did it on purpose," I said.

"People do," he said.

"Do what?" Grace said, looking up at us.

"She knew we would save her," he said.

The desire to escape the self, to become one with water. I knew that pull. Those long black months after losing my parents, the quarry was there, waiting for me.

Andy gazed down to the gorge. I followed his eyes.

I thought of the woman who drowned at the quarry, the weight of rock pulling her downward, anchoring her pain, releasing it.

"You don't know that," I said finally.

"Know what?" said Grace, tugging Andy's jacket. She turned to me. "Cat?"

He poked his daughter's belly. "Know how to eat doughnuts. Lots and lots of doughnuts."

After our day of sightseeing, when we got back to the apartment I saw a red flash on the answering machine. I turned down the volume, pressed *play*, and listened. Aunt Doris.

"She knows I'm here, right?" Andy said, flipping through the newspaper, the Books section.

"No," I said in a hush so Grace wouldn't hear. She was sprawled on the living room floor watching *The Simpsons*. I finished pouring her glass of chocolate milk.

"So I'm a secret?"

"No… it's just…" I stared at the milk bubbles. I was afraid to see his face.

I wanted to see Aunt Doris, but seeing her would mean facing this, this place I was in—neither here nor there. I could live in this gap but I didn't want to talk about it, I didn't want it questioned. She wouldn't see what I saw—this man, this love.

"I don't know what to say, exactly. Besides, Grace is here."

"And Grace will be gone. And she'll call again. You have your own life. Remember that. You don't need to explain it to anyone."

Linda was someone else on my list to catch up with. She too had left messages. She had yet to meet Andy, but knowing what I did know about her and Dad provided a margin of ease. Our growing relationship had survived the tremors and cracks of my father's adultery. Linda had given me back pieces of him.

And then she had met Jack.

"That's great," I said when she first told me the news during one of our weekend brunches. I was leaving soon for overseas. Was that why she told me? I'd mirrored her smile, but my insides churned. I saw the infatuation on her face— her green eyes freshened with light.

After that middle-of-the-night numbing moment, after the OPP knock on my bedroom door when I was informed of the fatal accident, it was Linda I phoned. She drove in the early morning hours to be with me in her stricken state—one I couldn't see at the time beyond my own.

Alone in the living room after the funeral, just the two of

us, she picked up my high-school grad photo—the one sitting on the TV—blew off the dust, and said ever so casually, "You look like a deer in headlights."

A current of knowing came blasting through, an inner truth: *I was the deer he swerved to miss that night. I was the sacrifice.* Somehow I knew this. Death was the only way he could let me go. Her sudden words made me see that. *A deer in headlights.* They unhooked the unsaid.

Mornings Andy worked on poems, Grace prepared for the eleven-plus exam she'd be taking in the fall for admission into Grammar School. It was the same test Andy had passed when he was her age, though barely. Grammar School was his daily refuge from the paramilitary groups that bred in the testosterone haunts of the largest housing estate in Western Europe. *UFF*: Ulster Freedom Fighters. *KAI:* Kill All Irish. He couldn't hide his school uniform, though he hid his new passion, one brought on by a charismatic English teacher.

"Mr. Nelson changed my life and he had no idea. I sat in the back with my mates pretending not to listen to Keats and the rest of them—took it in like a sponge."

"Wish I'd had a teacher like that," I said.

"Cat," said Grace, hugging me. "You *are* a teacher like that. Here." She handed me another completed paper.

I marked her mock tests and helped her with math, her weakest subject.

"Maths, Cat!" she said, teasingly. "Not *math.*"

For a reward we took her to the Games Room. Her favourite was Ms. Pacman. She loved dodging the little ghosts. Sometimes Andy won, sometimes Grace won. When she did win she'd do this little dance like her Manchester United hero, David Beckham, her sneakered feet stamping the cement floor, her father smiling at what he'd created.

I marvelled at that tricky balance. She never initiated his mask of pain, that black curtain that set his features to the dark place, which so often happened when I said or did something he didn't like. Even when playing a simple game of cards, Andy hated it when I won—attributing my win to luck, never skill or strategy. (And hated it when I pushed back: "Aren't we the sensitive one?")

He loved his daughter. I could see it in his focused attention—what I used to have—that gaze of fatherly pride.

I stared at Grace. *I will never feel that for you.*

Pinball was my game. Butting silver balls by the bat of an arm. *Ding-dong-ding.* A firing field of electronic lights like mad neurons in the brain.

Keep your eye on the ball.

I strained to hear.

Mother's words came back to me, but not her voice.

We had time for one more outing before she left, and Grace chose the zoo. Back home, she'd been to the one in the cut of Cave Hill, the landmark that had inspired Swift's image of Gulliver on his back, tied down by Lilliputians, his prone body—the very profile of it—there in the shape of the land.

"This zoo's ginormous!" Grace said, looking up at the giant map past the entryway where I'd purchased our family ticket.

We saw bats in their den of darkness, their folded wings like macabre leather flowers. We saw polar bears, sleek and smooth in their thick white coats as they swam in their fake sea. We saw penguins arrowing through icy waters, popping out like toast. And when we walked back outside, we saw a tiger in a field, off in the distance. Eyes aimed at Andy, the big cat came sauntering towards us and followed his stride along the chain-link fence. When Andy turned, she turned. When he turned again, she turned again. Back and forth they shadowboxed until Grace said, "Dad! You're teasing her. Catch yourself on!"

Only then did he stop.

It took him days to settle after Grace's departure. He could no longer watch *The Simpsons* or walk by the Games Room. I tossed out reminders: the carton of chocolate milk and box of Cap'n Crunch cereal. Eventually he did get back to working on old drafts and writing new ones while I taught the grade I hated.

Line by line, like a bricklayer, that's how Andy worked. Methodical. Analytical. Plotting a path to a destination, knowing one line will eventually reveal the end, the full-stop completeness of *done*.

I had no time to write now, but when I did, I wrote in bursts. The flash of a line or image had to be written down quickly or I lost the thread. Then I followed that thread—no, was led by it. Internal music led the way. My senses, charged by external triggers, stoked my inner life. A watch. A worm. A dust devil. I followed each sign and wrote my surrender.

Thoreau's headstone, mottled by leaf light and shadow, made me think: *Solas agus scáth*. Sun and shadow. One of the few Irish Gaelic phrases I remembered from my time overseas. My parents' stones weren't covered by shade. They shone under the light.

"This is what matters, Cat." Andy rested his hand on his hero's headstone. "*The mass of men lead lives of quiet desperation.*" He was looking at me now. "You think Mira knows that? All about the money, the car, the fancy house. You know what I'm talking about. You get what I'm saying."

Heat travelled through my eyes into Andy's like a circuit. "Yes," I said, cupping his hand, trapping the warmth from the headstone.

All the money in the world couldn't bring back my parents. Death takes you away from love, but love brings you back.

With the school year finished, I was free to return to Northern Ireland, but Andy wanted to visit America first. He wanted to see where his hero came from before our departure.

Previous visitors to Thoreau's grave had left an array of small offerings—pebbles and trinkets and wildflowers, purple vetch, goldenrod, black-eyed daisy. We left nothing behind but our fingerprints.

Andy's boyhood dream had become reality. I'd made that happen. Me. Back in our Concord hotel room, unplanned and natural, we came together.

I could hear Andy talking to the bartender as I looked out the window onto the main street of Amherst, at the people coming and going on this hot humid afternoon in this quaint colonial town we'd come to visit for the day. His brogue always triggered intrigue. It happened in Canada, but it was happening more frequently here.

"On the house," Andy said when he set the Guinness on the Miller High Life mats. We raised our glasses and clinked.

From Emily Dickinson's pristine hymn-book house to this dank and cheesy sports-bar slice of America, from the sublime to the ridiculous, here we were, toasting again.

"High Life, my arse." He looked around. "Art in the slops is more like it. Hey, that's not bad. Where's your pen, Cat?"

I handed him the pen from my money belt; he wrote the words down on the beer mat and passed them both back. "Can't believe I forgot my notebook in the room."

We continued drinking at the sports bar, talking about the famous homestead, her sleigh bed and small writing desk and that replica of one of her fascicles, handwritten poems bound with red yarn, her loopy handwriting and frenetic dashes.

I tried to forget the sexual frisson I'd witnessed between the curvy blonde tour guide and Andy. Whenever she spoke to the group while guiding us through the ochre-coloured brick house, she focused on him. Or had I imagined it?

When Andy returned with another free round he said, "Come on, we're moving to the back. Paddy wants to play."

I sat on a stool, my back to the wall, after shaking the bar owner's tough-skinned hand. Coloured balls ricocheted across the pool table. Andy rolled his eyes and the side of his mouth twitched. He stood back from the table and held his pool stick like a rifle, like a man in a duel.

"Your go, mate," he said, his eyes on his opponent.

Paddy's hair shone garish orange under the dim fluorescent light. He chalked his cue and chalked it again before blowing at the end. We all have our rituals to set us on track. Andy sharpened pencils, even though he used a pen. And he had to have a glass of water beside him—ice cold, a big glass—and God forbid any barking dogs, that sound drove him crazy.

"Best two out of three?" Andy said when he lost the game.

Paddy smiled. "*Chucky ar la.*"

"No surrender," said Andy, putting the balls back in the triangle. "How you doing over there, Cat? Another pint?"

When Andy turned the car around in the direction we'd just come from, our headlights hit the same stand of trees, tall like a thicket of giant pine soldiers. Eddies of stout sloshed through me and into my dry-heaving mouth—I opened the car door, the interior light dinging, and leaned out.

"Jesus, Cat!" Andy pulled onto the pebbled shoulder.

The night slid up my throat, past my lips, and out in warm soupy chunks.

"Cat!"

A siren blared and lights flashed behind us. Andy shouted, "Close the door!" He wiped my mouth with a Kleenex. He always kept one in his pocket, what men with children do. "You're okay. I'll handle this."

My head buzzed with confusion. A flashlight glared through the car exposing all.

"Sir, your licence," said the heavy-set officer, peering in.

Andy reached into his back pocket and pulled out ID.

"Step out of the car, sir."

I craned my neck to see what the officer was making Andy do. Touch his finger to his nose. Walk in a straight line. He'll be fine. It's me who's over the limit. How many pints did I have? I had no idea.

"Come with me," he said to Andy.

I could no longer see him, hear him.

"Miss," the officer said after opening my door.

"Our car…"

"Won't be going anywhere."

Tears clouded my vision. I wiped my nose with the Kleenex Andy had given me.

"You're not fit to drive either. I'm taking you both to the station."

Andy was already in the cruiser, handcuffed in the back.

"They can't do anything. I refused the breathalyzer."

He wanted to say more but the heavy-set officer had slipped behind the steering wheel. I set my hand on Andy's knee.

"Our car—"

"They're impounding it. He's taken the keys."

"No…"

"It'll be okay… we'll be okay…"

I couldn't connect to his words. I could only connect to the word *why*. Why did we go to the sports bar in Amherst? Why did we drink Paddy's free pints? Why did Andy challenge him to a game of pool?

They took his wallet and shoelaces, his fingerprints and then mug shot. They had him in a room behind glass. When I leaned forward on the foyer bench, I saw the back of his head. And then he was gone and there was nothing to do but try to pry something out of the bony gum-chewing officer behind the front desk.

"Would you please tell me what's happening?"

"Look, miss, he needs to be retained for the night. Standard procedure with impaired drivers who refuse the breathalyzer. Is there someone you can call?"

"We're not from here."

"He'll be out in the morning."

"Providing he keeps his mouth shut," said the heavy-set officer upon re-entering reception. "Stu will order you a taxi."

"No," I said. "I'm not going anywhere."

I returned to the bench, determined to keep watch, but a wave of tiredness took over and my eyelids pressed heavy. I bunched my money belt into a pillow, lay down, and slept in the open as the homeless do.

"Pet."

I opened my eyes. The first thing I saw—him standing over me.

"You're here," I said, standing up. I pressed myself into his chest, felt the heat and hold of his heartbeat.

"And how much do they fine me? Everything in my wallet. You have your Visa with you?"

I unzipped my money belt to check for the gold card and out fell the bar mat with Andy's words: *Art in the slops.*

He picked it up and pitched it against the wall. "*Eejits.* Come on."

A different officer drove us to the lot where the Honda was impounded. I wanted to ask Andy what had happened in the cell and what would happen next, but I knew now wasn't the time. After paying the fine, we found our car, and when I opened the passenger door the memory of last night came spewing out—flakes of dry vomit stickered the floor mat. The curdling stench permeated.

We cranked down the windows.

By the time we arrived back in Concord, to our clean hotel room, I knew where we stood. Andy would appear in court in three days.

We needed a lawyer.

Andy paced the floor of our box-shaped hotel room while I sat on the double bed, pillow to my chest like a lifejacket, the bed like a floating raft.

"What'd you go and open the car door for?"

"I… I couldn't help it."

"Yeah, yeah. Bloody Paddy. He set us up. He called the peelers."

He stopped pacing.

From the re-jigging of his features it seemed he'd encountered a new thought, one with hope.

"I'll call my mate Duncan. He used to be a lawyer. He'll know what to do."

I had yet to meet Andy's childhood friend from Rathcoole, but I knew they went to university together. When Duncan joined a prestigious law firm, he couldn't control his drinking; it got out of hand. "Lost his licence to practise," Andy said. "He became a lost man."

How will a lost man help us? I wanted to ask. But I didn't.

Andy dialled Duncan's number and told him the story. I didn't have to hear Duncan's voice to know things weren't looking any better.

Andy put down the phone.

"Well?" I pushed the pillow away and uncurled my legs to shake out the pins and needles.

"We face court and risk a heavy fine and God knows what else, or we head for the border and say our goodbyes to America."

"What do you mean *goodbyes*?"

"Ditch the joint and never come back."

"Forever?"

"*Finis.*"

There was something appealing about this. Get in the Honda and drive—away from Massachusetts, the state with the silly logo: *The Spirit of America*—and escape like the criminals we were.

"Let's," I said.

We met the Concord lawyer in his downtown office the following day. Scott Macintyre. A thin forty-something man with greying blond hair. When he looked down to write, his part shone under the fluorescent light like a landing strip.

"The judge will set the fine, suspend your licence, but once paid, you're free to go. You," he said, looking at me, "will do the driving. You have the money to pay for this, right?"

"More money," I said as I drove us back to the hotel.

"Go on. Make me feel shittier. Leave me in America. I'll make my way."

I shook my head. "Andy, I didn't mean that."

He stared out the passenger window.

"Andy?"

He wouldn't look at me.

I turned to the road, the tree-lined streets. *He'll come back. He always does. You just have to wait.*

She nagged him and I didn't do that. I accepted him as he was. Something I could do, accept. I'd never been the rebel. The energy inside didn't work that way. It wanted to shape things into rhythms and patterns, like the quilts my mother made. Square by square she stitched them together—calico green, gingham green, plain green. It was crucial for her to complete the quilts for my bedroom in time, to have her only child coated in green each night before falling asleep, before she settled beneath her own green.

Andy stood at the bedroom door of the apartment gripping the knob, nervously turning it back and forth, creating a staccato click beneath the hammer of falling rain. It didn't need to be turned; the door was wide open.

"You're still coming back with me, aren't you?"

I put down the book I wasn't reading on the unmade futon. Tornley's nature poems fluttered shut. I shimmied aside to give Andy room but when my elbow hit the wall, I moved back to claim my space.

He stood there watching me.

"I don't know," I said.

A deeper exhaustion had taken over since our return from the States. I thought I'd known what tiredness was, but this was different—an exhaustion that wasn't from grief. My body had gone to a slower register and my mind was taking more time to arrange the pieces of the ever-expanding puzzle of this. What *was* this?

"Cat," he said. He was sitting on the futon now, his tanned legs stretched out, his lower back pressed against my upper calf. I still hadn't moved. "No one will love you like this."

I stared at his khaki shorts. When we'd first arrived in Canada he'd been shocked by the frigid cold.

"Wait till summer, the incredible heat," I'd said. "You'll be wearing shorts."

"Shorts? Shorts are for pansies."

He slid his hand along my bare leg. I knew that touch, what that touch led to.

There were tears in his eyes. They hadn't fallen yet but were forming there like they were in mine—a cloud of rain, the rain outside, drumming the roof, streaking the windows. The weather was in our eyes.

"We can't part," he said. "You know that, right? We have to see this out."

IV

She wouldn't let him back in the house. She said no to his getting his things. She was changing her name back to her maiden name—Dunne, as in *done with you, boy.*

The plan, our ridiculous plan—to settle in slowly and help Mira adjust to this triangle we were living inside, while Andy and I found a place and eased into life before proceeding with the divorce—came to a slamming halt. I listened to her new-found voice—heard it blasting through the pay phone at the Belfast airport, the roaring pitch of it—and watched Andy's complexion turn the shade of red apples.

"Hoorbeg," he said, and slammed down the phone.

After checking the want ads at the back of the *Belfast Telegraph* we found a cottage for rent on the other side of the Lough. "We can bring cash over with your Visa." He folded the newspaper for easy viewing and dialled the number on the airport pay phone. "Grand," he said. "We'll take it."

A black taxi took us there. We sat silent in the roomy back-seat, oblivious to the cabby's mindless ramblings, his brogue as stiff as liquor, like something I ached for. Our heads were spinning—*what to do, what to do*—as we drove from the greens of County Antrim towards the greens of County Down.

"We have each other," Andy said, patting my knee.

The morning fog sat thickly around us, thick like our jet-lagged shock.

She didn't want him back. This was good news. Had she been planning this all along, even before his departure?

Andy clenched his hands. "She better let me see the girls. Jesus, if she touches my work…"

All the things he'd taken for granted tumbled out in mutters as we drove past the city limits. Samson and Goliath, the giant yellow cranes of Harland & Wolff, the famous shipyard, came into view, breaking the skyline.

She was those cranes and we, her sinking *Titanic*.

The cottage couldn't have been more idyllic. Ceramic jugs and porcelain dogs on shelves, country plates on walls and a hodgepodge of furniture ready to receive a young couple, their faces glowing like the bands on their newlywed fingers, eager to rush upstairs and whip off each other's clothes to consummate their love on the double bed.

"Andy?" I said, touching his arm, wanting to tell him this.

"Wait till she hears where we're staying. Money. Always on about money." He smiled as he looked up at me. "And who ends up living along the Golden Mile?"

No colour-coded curbstones in this part of Northern Ireland, just Prods and Catholics living side by side in stately houses in a place where money trumped religion.

He got quiet after that. The whole evening. I let him have his quiet.

"I'm a terrible father," he said, staring at the bedroom carpet, the shaggy strands.

I put down my book. "Andy—"

"Just like my da."

"No, you're not. We're here, aren't we?" I leaned across the bed to touch his shoulder. "He stayed in South Africa."

Andy pulled away as if I'd caused him pain.

"Go back to her then." It was out of my mouth before I could stop it. I held my breath.

He looked up but not at me. "You think I could do that? You think I came this far to do that?"

"You're not a terrible father, Andy. The girls love you. There's the proof. Mira knows that. We'll get into a routine. Families split up." I moved closer but didn't touch him.

"Families," he said, putting his arm around me. "You're my family."

I was sitting on the wing-backed chair in the lobby of the Culloden Hotel, the closest drinking establishment within walking distance from our rented cottage, while Andy stood talking to Mira on the pay phone. Culloden, another battle. We walk over lost blood without knowing it.

There, on my right, in the ornate room, through the glass cabinet, a mirror. *Hello, adulterer.*

I shuddered.

An ugly word, *adulterer.* Its stuttering end like an exhaust-pipe choke or an idle-to-dying motor. Yet it had the word *adult* in it.

Mom never told me what it was to become a woman. She let a doctor's pamphlet do the work, leaving me with the message: *be wary of your changing body.* So I cringed at the teenage wetness between my legs, inserted a tampon to stop it, stop this foreign re-circuitry.

And when I asked, what's French kissing? she stubbed her cigarette out in the ashtray, the smoke tendrils disappearing like my question. What is it? I repeated. *A kiss.* But why French? Do you like it? *Some women do.* She lit another cigarette. *You don't have to like it.*

On shelves in the glass cabinet that reflected my face sat rows of rubber ducks, signed in black ink by the rich and famous. Tom Jones. Billy Connolly. Bono. Proof they'd slept here, shit here, pissed here, perhaps even puked in this five-star hotel before cleaning up to face the parade of strangers with a kick in their step and a winning smile.

"Cat," Andy said with a rush of relief when he finished talking. "We're seeing the girls this weekend but I'll need to pick them up." He scratched his head. "We need a car."

He decided against buying the used Honda I'd spotted in the lot but he didn't say why. I didn't want to be the cause of more stress, so I didn't ask him why. We bought a Toyota instead, a new model, one with a roomy back seat for the girls. He was driving it now.

I set four plates on the cottage table, plus cutlery, napkins, and a bottle of red sauce for the take-away he'd be returning with—chicken nuggets and chips, their favourite. I took a deep breath.

So much had changed since I'd last seen Grace, and yet our time in Canada was not that long ago. Her *SWAK*-stickered letters kept arriving right up until our last week in the apartment. Would I see her mother's wrath in her sweet young face when she arrived at the cottage door? How would Chel react?

The door swung open. "Cat!"

I stood from the chair and Grace came running into my arms. I exhaled a long sigh and squeezed her in. Chel came running behind and joined our growing hug, the duet of their giggles lifting me up.

The cottage was quiet again with the girls' absence. Andy was upstairs, stretched out on the bed trying to write to meet his looming deadline, when the Education Association's new course catalogue arrived with the morning paper. *Open me, adulterer. Have a look.*

My hand blocked her face as if trying to protect me. I moved it aside. She was eyeing me now. Bold. Direct. A knowing expression in her half-smile. Her long straight hair cut short and trendy, triggering me to think—*Is that her? Mira Dunne.* Meaning, that wasn't her. We'd made her into a new woman.

"Andy?"

He didn't answer.

"I'm going for my run now."

The air was still moist from the rain. It cooled my skin like a damp cloth, a healing cloth. I wrapped my jacket around my waist and began jogging along the side of the road, the wrong side of the road, until I remembered where I was.

I passed rolling fields hedged in by hawthorn, fuchsia, and gorse. The green fields were weighed down by the grass-chewing sheep, cloud-shaped sheep like the ones in County Antrim. I jogged faster to clock time, to clock myself out of time and into the flow where the humming happened and the worrying stopped, *faster, faster*—I slipped into a core of oblivion and there it was, off in the distance, what I needed to see, what I ached to see—the endless blue water, the blue horizon.

Andy was shaking with cold when he woke me up in the middle of the night, though it wasn't cold in the rented cottage. The shaking was something else. He'd come out of a nightmare but the nightmare was still in him, circulating the imagery from the dark closet of his mind. What can I do? What can I do to help you? *Hold me*, he said. How small he seemed. How loose and fragile, as if his big-shouldered body were coming apart. He leaned into the weight of me, there on the double bed, the darkness shuddering through him. He held onto my strength while I rubbed the nightmare out of him. *What happened? Are you okay?* A strange whimper emerged from his throat, an animal gasp. And then he let go and I knew it was gone.

The layout of the house had a '70s feel. Split-level and so much light, dust particles twitched through the sunbeams. *We can be home here,* I thought. Our steps echoed through the vacant rooms. The view to the sea was the opposite from where I lived in Carrickfergus and so high up the sea, off in the distance, was like the backdrop of a movie. This could be our new home. County Down. Martello. Same name as the tower Joyce had lived in.

We put in an offer.

I had the money wired over. We paid in cash.

We moved from our little rented cottage to this split-level house. Andy relished the prestigious address. A moneyed home wasn't my motivation; distance was key—close enough for Andy to have access to the girls, far enough from Mira and Islandmagee gossip.

Andy returned from the bar with his pint and set it on the beer mat. His third or fourth?

I sipped my water. "You had the nightmare again last night."

He eyed my glass. "You're no fun anymore. Where's my Dublin girl?"

"She's here."

"Hardly. At least I don't hide this like your dad," he said and sipped, "and head off to Buffalo."

"Nana's birthday's coming up too." Dad and Nana's birthdays were only three days apart.

"From what you've told me, she doesn't deserve a card."

The last time I mentioned Nana we were sitting at this very table at the Cultra Inn. Every autumn when her neighbour's maple tree shed its leaves on her back lawn, Nana raked them up and tossed them back over the fence without saying a word.

I fingered the condensation on my glass. "One time when I was playing dress-up, Nana called me to dinner... I was changing into my other clothes when she came looking for me. There were only a few clothes on the floor—it wasn't that bad. She was furious. I told her I'd clean it up after and she just glared. *Now,* she said. *Clean it up now.* I started to cry. She didn't care. She stood there watching me."

"She's like my da," Andy said, cradling his Guinness.

I touched his hand.

"It's okay, Cat. He's dead to me now."

Are you sure? I wanted to ask. He rarely talked about his father, but from the pieces he'd randomly dropped, I had a fierce image of him: powerful, demanding, intimidating, neglectful of his family's needs. "He was there and then wasn't," Andy had said. "Out drinking with his mates, coming home drunk, Mum up waiting for him. My first memory's my parents fighting, their voices through the walls while I stared at the mobile hanging above my bed. I remember wheels... trains, maybe? But they were too far away to make them spin."

They were estranged now. As hurtful as Nana was, I couldn't shut her out of my life. I saw what estrangement did to family. The pain it caused. Aunt Doris and Dad not talking for years—not talking forever because now he's dead.

I looked out the rain-streaked window. The light from the parking lot gave a moody glow. "We never did go to the grave. You never saw where they were buried."

"We'll go. Next time we're in Canada. Own Sound."

"Owen," I said. "*Owen* Sound."

"You're going to have to let them go. You have a life here now."

"Life? How do I have a life? I can't work here. I can't travel with an out-of-date passport. My time's up, remember? What if Mira finds out?"

"And scupper what she's got going here? You've been generous with money. We've needed it to build *this*. Once the divorce is through, she'll have nothing over us. We just have to wait. Cat?"

I blinked back the tears. "I don't want to go back."

"You think, after all this, I'd let that happen?"

I turned away and looked at the floor.

"Hey," he said, squeezing my wrist. "Give us a smile."

His eyes were crossed, his mouth contorted.

"That's my girl."

I kept my hands on the wheel, my eyes on the rain-streaked road. The tarmac was cloaked with low-hanging fog. It was hard to see the yellow lines. It wasn't safe for me to drive here without a license, but it was only a short distance.

Andy rested his hand on my knee. He slid it higher.

"Not now. I need to concentrate."

"Ah, come on. Sing with me. Sing *cockles and muscles, alive, alive, oh.*" He squeezed my upper thigh.

"Stop it."

"Fine," he said, pulling away. "Go back then and get yourself a nice Canadian boy." He pushed the passenger seat all the way back, crossed his arms and closed his eyes. The smell of stale Guinness from his mouth. He was quiet but I knew he wasn't sleeping. He lurched forward and turned the radio on full blast.

The loud music was like a slap in the face. I willed myself not to hear it.

I didn't see anyone about my grief after Mom's death. I had Dad then. Only after Dad's death did I see a counsellor. It was Linda who'd suggested I see someone. Month after month she'd said this gently until her message finally got through. I had no idea what to say or how to prepare. I sat in the waiting room, self-cornered and looking out, adjacent to nobody, flipping through *Time*'s glossy pages.

"Caitlin?"

I turned to the source—soft feminine features and caramel-coloured eyes that signalled: *I care.*

Ms. Moore sat in the chair directly across from mine. The room smelled like the potpourri in the waiting room but I didn't see a bowl, just a still life of flowers nailed to the wall, three yellow roses. She knew about the back-to-back deaths, so that's where she started. *Must be hard...* something like that. I remember nodding. The way her turtleneck folded over her stomach, it looked like she was pregnant. I wanted to put my hand there, to feel life's kick, but I knew it was an illusion.

Session after session, buried thoughts came out of my mouth as if she were a magician pulling a chain of knotted rags. *My fault she got cancer, in her thirties when she had me... never got to the hospital in time to say goodbye, I knew she'd die Christmas Day, I had this feeling... my fault Dad died in the car accident... I knew he shouldn't go to Buffalo that night... I should've listened to that voice inside me... I should've stopped him... I could've stopped him.*

I learned what people learn in grief, that loss has many stages, that it comes in waves and crawls back into desert, how pain—the ache—never goes away though the sting lessens somewhat. You must learn to live on with grief. In your body, your bones, your blood.

Turns out this was "normal." Nothing Ms. Moore hadn't heard before. My weekly airing was there in the curve of her belly, until that moment when she stood from her wing-backed chair and I watched my life flatten out of her.

I remember that last session. When it came to personality types, my ability to take things as they come plus my deep well of patience and my preference for being a watcher rather than a participant put me in the "adaptive category." I thought of an oyster, that sand-bedded sea creature, silent and closed, impearling grit into precious.

Andy liked to laze in bed before he started his day, so it made sense for me to bring him a cheese toastie, milky tea, and Twix bar.

Once he was out of bed I flicked the crumbs off his side, collected dirty dishes, tossed the chocolate wrapper in the bin (plus any balls of dried tissue).

Martello Park hadn't sunk under his skin, not yet, like Islandmagee had done. The poems he was writing, when he was writing, were like stars that couldn't form a constellation. What he needed was a unifying theme and time was running out and her demands for money increasing.

"You'll leave me," he said one night, staring into the fire. "You'll go back to Canada."

"Stop saying that. It's like a curse. Does it have to be a spring launch? Ask for more time."

He put his hand over his heart. "There's nothing left to pull out."

"You have lots of poems now."

"Not enough to make a book that matters."

I poked at the coal to trigger the embers. "We're in this house too much. Tollymore. Didn't you say you'd take me there again?" I moved towards him. He put his hands on my waist and guided me down on the floor. I cradled my head on his lap.

The next day after our visit, all that green forest air in our lungs, an idea came to him, an imaginary venture—Thoreau visits the Mourne Mountains. And his face, like mine, lit up again.

"Told you the money would start coming in. Listen to this," Andy said. "You listening?"

I sat down on the wooden chair in his study. The paper in his hand was so thick I couldn't see through to the ink. My father would know the quality of that paper.

He cleared his throat and paused.

"Come on, Andy."

"Okay okay. *Your endeavour is a noble one and I would be honoured to participate but I am trying to claw back tiny pieces of myself that I have already committed to.*" He put the letter down. "Not every day you hear from a former Poet Laureate," he said, rolling his chair into a half-spin.

"He got back to you quickly. What about Tornley?"

Neither of us had spoken to Tornley since our return.

"You're right. He'll know what's happened by now."

"He probably knew all along, don't you think?"

Andy didn't answer. He asked me to leave the room while he made the call to invite him to the literary festival he was organizing. I was tempted to stand in the hallway and listen. Wasn't Tornley my friend too? I thought of something Andy had said that day he was so angry at me for accepting that ride back to Carrickfergus. "Tornley knows the complications of the heart. Don't let that wedding ring fool you."

I took a seat in the living room and stared out the window. The SeaCat was heading to Scotland again. The risen wake behind the fast-moving boat was like a seabird ruffling her feathers—release the bad energy to move forward, shake the bad energy out. I shook my arms but nothing happened.

"Another yes!" Andy shouted as he made his way down the hallway. He raised his fist as he entered the living room. "Torn loves the idea. That'll show Mira. Thinks I've committed literary suicide. Wait till she reads about the festival in the *Belfast Telegraph*." He pulled me up from the easy chair and hugged me tightly like my father used to do when he was high and happy after securing a big envelope account.

"How about a cuppa, Cat?"

"Sure. I'll make some tea."

"And Twix?"

"Yes, Twix."

"Lovely," he said, and sat down in the chair I'd been sitting on. He turned on the telly.

I set his snack on the table beside him.

"Did you remember to put the milk in first?"

I nodded.

"By the way, Tornley was asking for you. He says *tickety-boo*."

I sat at my desk, pen in hand, my notebook open and blank. It was my turn to feel down. I wasn't supposed to feel this way. You have your man, a home with a stunning view—what more do you want? But Andy's recent high had tipped me low, the anchored half of a seesaw.

Through the wall between us I heard the clacking of his keyboard, the *grrr* of his printer. His bright face appeared at my half-open door. He pushed it open. "Listen to this." He read his poem, his latest draft. "What do you think?"

"It's good," I said.

"Yeah?"

"Really good."

The next day when he was ready to share his work, I wasn't sitting at my desk.

"Cat?"

I was upstairs in the girls' room under Grace's moon-and-stars duvet, surrounded by her zoo of stuffed animals, trying to nap, to take away the tiredness weighing me down. The scent of her red-cheeked youth, embedded in the sheets and pillow.

"Moneybags Maharg," Grace called me, because she heard Andy call me that. Funny at first, the alliteration, the way it rolled off the tongue. I had what he didn't have—money. I thought back to his place of origin—Rathcoole. How proud he was when he showed me. I remember thinking: Here is where you come from? An inner-city estate close to Belfast Lough but not near enough to see it, a place where families and broken families lived side by side in two-up and one-downs or stacked on top of each other in high-rises. Hiding from the milkman when he came to collect money—Andy, his brother and his mother crouched behind the sofa, playing a game that wasn't a game. As eldest, Andy had the head start in life. His voice came first. All his brother had to do to communicate was to point or make some other kind of signal that only Andy understood. He then translated their non-verbal wants into words for the confused adults, including their mother. This went on for such an extended period of time there was talk the young Evans boy was "thick as two short planks." Eventually someone caught on to what Andy was doing—taking over—a teacher or neighbour, Andy never said, but he was told to stop. "Let him speak for himself, son," said his mother.

But Grace didn't ask me for money. She always asked Andy because (this I know) Mira told her to. "You want a new bike? Ask your Craigavad da. He'll give it to you." And what I'd done, what I'd been part of—breaking up a family—could appear to be fixed when I passed him another cheque. And Grace would smile. And Grace would be happy.

"What are you doing up here?" Andy turned on the lights and sat on Chel's bed. "I was just on the phone with Patrick. He says we have enough funding for one more writer and I thought, you teach, you could do it. Get the students writing poetry, read some poems. How about it, Cat?"

I stood by the living room door, my hands on my hips.

Andy muted the telly's volume, *The Match of the Day.* "What is it, Pet?"

121

I was about to say, *she won't listen to me*, because I thought he was talking to me, but then Chel pushed me aside, no, shoved me aside, and ran into the living room, straight into her father's arms, the cotton feet of her pink jimjams loose and elongated like twin flapping tongues as she rose high in the air like an airplane.

"Got ya," he said, holding her. "You wee hellion!"

She squealed when he put her down. "Again!"

This time she rose higher. Her fleshy arms, fully wide, her chubby hands stretched open. That stubborn ball of tightness I'd experienced when she refused to go to bed—gone.

She turned to see where I was, beside the crackling fire. She didn't have to say a thing, her look said all. She was getting back at me and she was savouring the moment. Just like her mother and her weekly demands. *You split up the family, Andy. Not me. And her.*

The house had fallen to quiet again. I could finally relax after another last-minute panic to find Chel's soother (under the sofa cushion, again). She was always losing it. That defiant, annoying sucking sound as her mouth moved in and out, in and out like a fish's. She was too old for it now but refused to part with it. Andy blamed the habit on her mother.

Mira.

That name infiltrated our house like a permanent ghost.

But I'd returned her daughters with the greatest care. I combed Chel's curls and wiped the chocolate from her mouth. I helped Grace with some last-minute maths homework. Educational costs had gone up with her attending Grammar School, but I gritted my teeth.

"It's only temporary," Andy said. "And you know I'll get good money for organizing the festival."

But he kept buying expensive hard-backed books, biographies of Auden and Yeats and MacNeice.

"Why not use the library?" I'd said the last time he purchased another signed first edition, gently so he wouldn't take it the wrong way. Anyone could get a library card, even an illegal alien like me. They never asked to see my passport.

"All right for some," he said, "but I need to *own* the book."

I went from room to room restoring order—straightened the girls' bed-making efforts, tossed out candy wrappers ("*Sweets*, Cat!") and plumped the pillows in the family room. I vacuumed the carpets, washed and dried dishes, tucked in chairs and wiped sticky fingerprints from all the glass doors. I had the house pristine perfect by the time Andy arrived back. He didn't notice.

The return to childless silence wasn't easy for him. That first hour was an unsettled one. He'd have the girls living here seven days a week if he could. Thankfully Mira did not want that.

Andy rang our neighbours' doorbell and they both came to the door. They took our coats and guided us into the living room, towards the blue flowery sofa and matching chairs. They poured us wine—Château Clerc Milon—an enviable terroir, so we were told. We'd been living next door for some time and only now had we accepted their dinner invitation—*we have to go, Andy. We can't keep saying no.*

Despite the time passing, they asked us politely, "Have you settled in okay?"

"Oh, yes," I said to our elderly neighbours, William and Geri. Andy simply nodded. I continued talking about the lovely sea view, lush back garden, the palm tree on our front lawn—so tropical!—thanks to the Gulf Stream, a stream of water inside water made route for warmth.

"Canada," Geri said, waving her manicured hands, the rusty brown matched her lipstick. "I used to live in Montreal."

"Really?" I said. "My dad was from Montreal."

"My first husband was a Canadian, like you. English speaking, not French… Banning English from signs. Who do they think they are, the French?"

William smiled and nodded at his wife. "It brought you back to Craigavad."

"Yes, honey. It did." She looked lovingly across the room at the fit bald man, then turned to us. "William and I knew each other years ago, at public school. We ran into each other again at the Royal Yacht Club."

William nodded.

Geri smiled. "I see the cutest girls running around on weekends." She looked at Andy sitting in the blue chair. "Are they yours?"

She'd slipped the question in so quickly I tried not to squirm. Andy gulped his wine like he was finishing a pint. I looked at William and Geri's barely sipped glasses. Mine, somewhere in between.

"Yes," he said, putting his empty glass down on the mahogany table, avoiding the coaster. He eyed the drink caddy. "Yous don't mind, do you?" he said as he made his way towards it.

William watched as Andy refilled his glass. I thought of Nana. William's eyes were round like hers. "Yous go right ahead," he said.

Was he mocking Andy? William had spoken so softly I couldn't be sure. No matter. Andy was fiddling with the decanter now, refastening the crystal lid.

He returned to his chair. We waited for him to say more. He didn't.

"Grace is the older one," I said. "She just started Grammar School. Chel, she's the youngest."

"Always sucking a soother, isn't she? So they don't live with you," Geri said.

"They do," Andy said. "On weekends."

"They're with their mother during the week," I said. "They're settled there—with school and friends—but they like it here."

"Two homes," said Geri. She sighed dramatically. "Such a different world these days."

"You're divorced," Andy said. "You know it happens."

"Andy," I whispered.

"Let's face it," he continued, "you marry young—too young—you pay the price."

"So," said William, "you're married now."

He meant us. I was sure of it. I hid my left hand. Would Andy get that?

"Something smells delicious," I said, sitting up, sniffing the air. "Do you need any help in the kitchen?"

"Oh no, dear," said Geri, standing up. She motioned for me to sit, to stay in place. The blue flowers in her wraparound dress matched the sofa like an accessory. "William, come slice the roast." She smacked her lips. "And there's Yorkshire pudding."

"You're in for a treat," said William. His shiny forehead caught the glow of the lamplight. "Geri's a fantastic cook."

"Oh, now," Geri said, waving her hands again. "Don't make me blush."

They left us alone as they clanked away in the kitchen.

"*Craigavad*. What a poser. It's Martello."

"Stop it. They'll hear you."

"They can't hear me. They're going deaf."

"Andy." I tried not to laugh.

"Jesus. They're old enough to." He finished his wine and stood with his glass in hand. "Don't worry," he said, watching me. "I'll wait for dinner."

His voice came back during dinner, as if the gravy-puddled slices of roast beef, the Yorkshire pudding, boiled peas and mashed potatoes, had unlocked his storytelling voice.

We'd given them a bottle of Merlot as a gift, plus a bouquet of yellow mums that Geri had since placed in a big blue vase. After another jokey hint from Andy, William uncorked the merlot. Only Andy drank from it.

"That wasn't so bad," Andy said an hour later as we walked up our slanted driveway towards the stairs. When we reached the landing, he put his arm around my shoulders. "Look at that," he said.

The Lough lay completely still, the surrounding lights reflected like inverted candles. The boats moved as rafts of light. It was the kind of peacefulness one finds with water. A soul of calm before the breeze blows it away.

Every writer showed up on time, a rarity I was told, and the young and hip headmaster, Patrick, was thrilled with the names stepping in and out of his classrooms. Knowing the value of a photo-op, he made sure shots were taken from all angles, for newspapers big and small, to show this school was on the rise.

I began carefully with the class I'd been assigned to, emphasizing play and discovery, the joy of words. After some rapid imagery exercises I got them writing free verse. I wanted them to avoid sappy singsongs. "Rhyming is hard. New rhymes, that is, ones that haven't been done before. Try to find your own music."

They loved hearing my accent. "You were a hit," Patrick said, when Andy and I said our goodbyes. Patrick's handshake was slick like his perfectly fitted suit. I couldn't imagine him wearing casual clothes like Andy—khaki trousers, button-down shirt, and brown brogues. "You must come back, you're a natural." He rubbed his clean-shaven face. "Ever thought of teaching full time?"

I am a teacher! But I held my tongue. It would only invite more questions, and I'd have to lie about being here illegally.

The following Saturday night, buoyed with optimism, Andy met up with Patrick at the Cultra Inn while I watched the girls. He had an idea to share with the young headmaster. Start a press, a literary press that produced beautiful books, and begin with an anthology of the writers who'd participated in the festival.

Patrick loved the idea.

Mira met someone at a Belfast art exhibition during an outing with a friend, that drama-class friend Andy had run into at the National Gallery of Ireland that day in Dublin when he pretended he didn't know me. He was handsome, this man, with a posh English accent. He engaged her attention with some harmless chit-chat which quickly turned into flirtation. When he asked for her number, Mira Dunne said *yes*.

He followed her up on that yes. Phoned her, asked her out, and out they went for a meal to a local pub, which just happened to be the place where Andy had ordered my first Guinness, the White Cliff Inn. She was smitten. Flowers and cards and so much attention. When I look back I can pinpoint when this all happened. The weekend notes she stuffed into the girls' overnight bags (sad plastic bags) carried a neutral air, less pointed and stinging.

But, like many men, once he got what he wanted, the game was over. She was mud in his hands, easy to mould, and his fingers were bored and sticky. His phone calls began to lose frequency, a slow dripless feed, until his lack of interest became official and he never called again.

She'd been in bed all day when it was time for Andy to pick up the girls, and the day before, she never did get out of bed—that's what Grace told her father when she and Chel hopped into the Toyota. Grace was in a flap about having to pack Chel's overnight bag. Did she get everything? When she checked the contents of the plastic bag, she realized she'd forgotten Chel's jimjams.

"I'll get them," Andy said. "Stay in the car."

He hadn't been in the house for months. He cringed at the changes. The sofa sat too close to the telly, and what a bad choice of yellow paint. He was tempted to take all the paintings—they were his after all—when he heard a stirring in the master bedroom.

"Grace, sweetie? That you?"

"It's me, M. You okay?"

He entered her room, their old bedroom, and there she was—her small body beneath the duvet covers, her pretty face propped up on the bunched pillows, her wide eyes red and teary. She told him everything about the man she'd met, which he later told me, which led to the parts above I imagined. My mind needed something to fill it—another Saturday night at home watching the girls while Andy was out with Patrick.

Wrapped in their moon-and-stars duvets, the girls had fallen asleep by the slow-burning fire. Grace's mouth—wide open and vulnerable. Chel's was corked with a soother.

The thought of Andy sitting by Mira's bedside—the matrimonial bed—listening to her story of recent heartbreak. *Consoling her.* What I thought, what I wanted, didn't matter.

I ran my fingers across the book's hardback cover and breathed in the new-book smell. *Duelling Words: an Anthology of Poetry*—and my words inside it.

My parents would never see my work and yet they were my work. Andy's parents, though still alive, wouldn't see his work either. His father, estranged. His mother—"She doesn't get this," he'd said when he passed me the anthology. She still lived in Rathcoole.

Side by side in a moonlit landscape the duellers stood. The light of the full moon rippled across the lake like a watery grave ready and waiting for the loser. White shirt, grey waistcoat, black trousers, and twin licks of moonlight on their black boots, they pointed their pistols upwards. No anger or fear in their faces. Everything about them was masked emotion. You had to look closely to see the hot-air balloon bracketed between the thin layers of cloud, what I loved best about the cover. Somebody was in there manning the flame, making a path through air, escaping.

We were watching *Coronation Street*, our plates on our laps. I smiled as I stirred the take-away curry to even out the sauce. He'll finally hear me read.

"I've been practicing the poems out loud. It's important to get the pauses, right? If you read too fast—"

Andy muted the volume.

"Cat, turns out we have enough readers for the launch."

I dropped my fork on the stirred mound. "What do you mean?"

He pushed a forkful of curry in his mouth.

"I thought you wanted me to read, Andy."

I waited for him to finish. Did he always chew so slowly?

"I do, you know that, but the timing isn't right." Then he pointed to the anthology he'd propped on my mother's lidded upright grand for easy viewing. Like the other treasured items I'd kept from the quarry house, the piano had been shipped across the Atlantic. I didn't want anyone playing Mom's piano. I wanted it closed like the coffin it was. He could easily see the book sitting there, see his hard work. His poems were in it too. "When you have enough strong poems we'll look at doing yours." He turned my way. "Come on, I feel bad enough. You're in the anthology, aren't you?"

"I don't get it," I said.

"You think I haven't thought about this? You want to talk, let's talk. I thought you understood."

"Understood what?"

"My publishing you, that's what. The pressure I'm under."

"You said you liked my poems."

"I do like them."

"But I was there too." I thought of Tornley and the other writers who'd visited the school that week for the festival, how exciting it was to be published with them.

"Right. And why were you there?"

"Is this some kind of payoff because I helped you fund it?"

"You know you'll get it back. Patrick gave his word."

"I'm not a vanity case, Andy." Or was I? Was I just some poet desperate to be published—anywhere by anyone—to see my name in print?

I picked up the book and leafed through it to find my poems, to rip them out, but before I could, he swiped it from my hands and grabbed my wrist. He stared at me, maintaining his grip, until I looked away and he finally let go.

Mom was dead by the time I discovered the abuse. But like other things I needed to know, my dreams—no, my nightmares—had already told me. My mother lying in the open-lid coffin wearing a white-wedding dress—ripped and tattered in places that revealed boils of pus and grey-black bruises, the dark blood caked into dried curdles and that hand, that beckoning hand, calling me closer. What did she want me to see?

We're keeping the coffin closed. We need to remember your mother as she was.

But who was she? A quiet woman who sat with her legs curled up, smoking her endless cigarettes, sewing her quilts and crafts, staring out at the quarry, at the white caps coming and going, the water turning from blue to black, absorbing the night as day by day her athletic body slowly betrayed her.

My parents could pretend they were married, both being born with the surname Maharg. They could lie to the world, to me, but not to Nana. She knew the man before my father. She'd been at their wedding in Owen Sound. She knew Dad, despite what he claimed, was never Mom's husband. Fate, when she took back her maiden name, gave them the same surname, not God.

He beat her on her wedding night and night after night. The snap of his leather belt, insertion of sharp things—that's what my mother's nursing-school friend told me Mom's first husband did when I tracked her down.

Alone in the living room, Andy in his study, I touched my arm where he'd grabbed it. No marks to signal pain, just freckles like my mother's arm. Brown stars of constellation.

Tornley took his place behind the podium after Andy's glowing introduction. After scanning the audience, the packed auditorium, he caught my eye in the third row.

"Why aren't you up here?" he said, tapping the anthology. "Why, I'll not read until Caitlin does."

I touched my chest. "*Me?*"

He nodded.

"You'll be grand," said a voice from behind. How I'd ached to hear that voice. Yet she wouldn't say *grand*, she'd say *great*. *You'll be great, honey.*

I set the open anthology on the podium. I didn't dare look at the far wall. When I finished with the last line of the last poem: *Grief is like waiting for fifty giant black kettles to boil*, only then did I look up. The audience clapped. I wanted to fall into that clapping and stay shielded there.

"Great," said the same female voice when I sat back down. *Don't turn and break the spell. Pretend she's here with you.*

Tornley resumed his place behind the podium. He chuckled. "And I have to follow that?"

I turned to the far wall. Arms crossed, features stiff, Andy stared straight-faced at me.

Crackers, cheese, and bottles of wine on one table, the anthology for sale on the other. I sipped the wine, warm cherry and leather notes in the Rioja that Tornley had given me.

"Caitlin," said Tornley, clinking my glass. "Well done."

"Thanks," I said, half listening. I couldn't locate Andy in the gathering crowd. "I was pretty nervous."

"You'd never know it."

I thought back to the moment I'd stood behind the podium, my heart like a wind-up toy. Couldn't the audience see that?

"I've been meaning to tell you about our workshop at Queen's," said Tornley.

A hand clutched my shoulder.

"She's on a roll with her poems now, Torn. You know what it's like." Andy released his grip and began caressing the middle of my back. He ended with his signature touch—a slow spiralling key. "We've got a good rhythm with everything going on—a press to run, more books to distribute."

"You're publishing more?"

"I've been corresponding with some Irish poets—"

"Really," said Tornley.

"Got the letters."

"Hmm," said Tornley. "Any other takers?"

"Well, there's you, of course," said Andy, winking. "We could publish your Iceland poems."

"Why, yes," said Tornley. He tugged his grey beard. "I'd be happy to send you something." He looked at his wine glass. "Time for a top-up."

I sipped and waited for Andy to speak.

"You read well," he said.

"You think so?" I smiled.

"But you got the poem wrong."

"What do you mean?"

"*Like* waiting. Grief *is*."

"I said *like*?"

"You did."

"I don't remember."

"Grief *is* waiting for fifty giant black kettles to boil. That's the line in the book."

"Is," I repeated.

When we'd first arrived back in Northern Ireland from our spell in Canada nobody from the Belfast literati approached Andy to see how he was doing, not even Tornley. They knew he was back. They'd see him browsing the aisles of Belfast bookstores. The most awkward encounters were with the less-talented poets like Sean McGinty, an up-and-comer who'd just published his first book after years of being a "promising" poet. Andy's absence had left open ground for weaker seeds to grow. Proof the Belfast imagination was like the warring colours on curbstones, everything tribal here.

Now that the press was official—the Mourne Press, head office Craigavad—Andy's meetings with Patrick became more frequent. Saturday night was the only night they could get together, so off they went to the Cultra Inn to work. They always held their meetings after meals so Andy could eat with me and the girls.

"Why can't you work here?" I asked one night.

He watched me scrape the rice bits off his plate into the bin under the sink. The kitchen window had a view to the back garden, the shouldering slope like a hill of green meadow, but the kitchen was so outdated, a muddy green from the '70s. I trained my eyes not to see it. Sometimes it worked.

"You know the girls won't leave me alone," he said, buttoning his leather jacket. "We'll never get any work done."

He headed to the front door. I followed him.

Grace ran out of the living room from her nest of pillows by the fireplace. "Da, don't go!" She crouched on the carpet and hugged his leg, his khaki trousers. He'd just opened the door so the cold blew in like a force, making me shiver.

Playfully dramatic, Grace squealed again, "Pleeeease!"

"Daaaa, don't go!" said Chel, jumping off the sofa. She mirrored her big sister's performance but instead of grabbing hold of his other leg, she aimed for the one Grace held onto. Grace nudged her little sister aside and Chel feigned hurt. She whined and cried like a wounded lamb. *Gurning*, Andy called it. The mess of noise I was left with.

"Read us that book again, Cat," Grace said later that night after I'd tucked them into bed. I knew it was her tactic to avoid sleep, but I didn't mind. I loved reading them stories. It was my favourite part of teaching too—story time.

Grace lifted *Tell Me the Colour of Love* from the table beside her. "This smell," she said, sniffing the hardcover. "I love how old it is."

Chel sat up in her twin bed. "Let me smell!"

Grace handed me the book and I let Chel smell it. "Yummy," she said, licking it as I held it.

"Chel! Don't wreck Cat's book!"

Chel giggled. "I'm a puppy," she said, whimpering. "No, a cat! Like you, Cat!" She licked the back of her hand and rubbed her face.

"Let's all be cats," I said and did the same. They were getting more excited, but I knew they'd soon reach their peak and the energy would wane.

They were both out cold before I finished reading the book.

I hadn't planned on keeping *Tell Me the Colour of Love*. At seven years of age I wanted to see love's colour.

We see colour with our eyes.
Only our hearts see love.
Heart, what colour do you see?
Tell me.
Why won't you tell me?

When it was time to return the library book I told Mom I'd lost it, but I knew where it was, in the bottom of my toy box. I thought if I read it slowly, carefully, *Tell Me the Colour of Love* would reveal the answer.

Perhaps I had to grow one more inch on the height chart to see love's colour. I could wait. Once I saw the colour of love, I'd return the book. Surely the printed page owed me that. The three big-headed children on the cover held pastel-coloured balloons on a hill of green meadow. Two girls and one boy. Their eyes, black dots. No mouths on their faces.

Without any mouths, how could they tell me?

I did a whole-body pout there in his study. A silent pout for him to notice.

for my family

I turned from the proof, the loose-leaf manuscript the Belfast printing press had mailed to our Martello address, and sat across from him, swivelling in his chair.

"What?" he said, tapping his desk with his chewed-up pencil. "It's the font, isn't it. Too small, you think?"

"No," I said, squirming in the wooden chair. "It's not the font."

He turned to the page in question. "You're in here," he said, pointing at the dedication.

"As family?"

He nodded.

Say it. Say what you think.

He continued staring at the dedication, but his mouth stiffened.

"She's your family," I said. "According to the law."

"Here we go…"

"What. Like people don't know we're together?"

"I need to respect my past. She's part of my manuscript."

"More than me, you mean."

"Come on. Think about the girls. If I put your name down here, I'm putting you first. We don't want to fire things up. A dedication like this could work for us."

I dedicated my thesis to you. Freely, openly.

"Cat?"

The first tear took me by surprise.

"Here," he said, pulling a Kleenex from his jeans pocket. "It won't always be like this. There'll be other books." He put his hand on the dedication page. "This should bear your name. We know it should. You're in here too. Can't you see that? Maybe you need to lie down. You look a little green." He walked around his desk and pulled me off the wooden chair, hugged me. "I'll make you a hot water bottle."

As I lay upstairs under the moon-and-stars duvet, I tried to understand my want. My name in his book would be a signal to everyone reading it: *this woman matters.*

Love has no colour. Love is a void. The black of dark.

I sat at my desk staring at the few lines I'd written—random, disassociated, no heartbeat in them, lines immersed in a flat line of silence—when I heard footsteps climbing the stairs to the front door. They stopped at the landing. I waited for the metal's squeaky hinge. No sound. Perhaps the postman was catching his breath while taking in the view—the rooftops of the neighbouring houses, the shimmering lough off in the distance—then came the familiar ping and plop as our bundle of mail dropped onto the doormat.

With Andy out of the house I couldn't resist the distraction. No, not distraction, temptation, for I knew I could let things sit.

The postman was already next door by the time I peeked out the window. Perhaps that's what I'll be when I'm finally able to work here legally—a postie. Be the bearer of daily news, from the irritating to the mundane to the soul-sucking painful.

I leafed through the stack. *Andy. Andy.* Bill. Flyer. *Andy.* Bill. My handwriting, a letter addressed to me.

Thank you for this opportunity to read your work. Though some imagery shows promise we found most of the lines flat. We encourage you on your writing path.

Encourage? Where's the encouragement?

Here I was in the land of poetry with endless time on my hands and I could barely write. Then when I did write, I wrote stillborn poems. Flat. No heartbeat in them. Dead babies. And there was Andy, riding high.

I leaned my head against the door's cool glass. I wanted to be that postie, on my way to the next house, drop and go, have no association, no connection to the words you carried, just keep on walking and walking in your weather-proof uniform until the load was empty.

I headed up the hill, my lungs full of salty sea air, my mind packed with the healing images from my seaside walk. Cormorants and kittiwakes and what appeared to be a rock until it bobbed up and dove under.

The car was in the driveway so I knew he was home. *Is that him at the window?* The glare from the setting sun made it hard to discern as I walked up the driveway's slope.

I opened the front door, my heart pounding from my two-step-at-a-time leap up the steps, and shouted, "I saw a seal!" I stood still to listen. No keyboard clicking. No television. No voice on the phone. Is he napping? "Andy?"

"In here," he said in a voice so low I barely recognized it.

I walked into the living room and stood by the unlit fireplace. He was sitting in his easy chair.

"Why are you sitting in the dark?" I reached for the lamp on the piano.

"Leave it," he said.

"What's wrong? Did something go wrong with your school visit?"

"Where were you?" he said, eyeing me—my face, my clothes. Up. Down.

"Out for a walk."

"And."

"And, what?"

"You saw a seal."

"My first." I smiled after I said that. He didn't smile back. "What is it?"

"I don't know. You tell me."

"I don't get—"

"You went down the trail. You have to go down the trail to see any seals."

"There was no one there. Just an old man walking his dog."

"Why not go down right now, then? It's getting nice and dark. You felt safe. Isn't that nice."

"Andy—"

"Meanwhile, I come home, I come home early—say no to the organizer, Ronnie, who wanted to buy me a pint, who wants to meet you by the way, so I can come home—to you—so we can go for a pint, together, and I come home to an empty house."

"I—I had to get out."

"No note. No nothing. But you saw a seal."

I grabbed the envelope I'd set on the mantelpiece and removed the letter. "They suck, see? They're flat."

He set the letter on his armchair and rested his forearm flatly over it.

He's read it already?

"This happens to writers. You need to get used to it."

"Used to it? You don't get them."

He smiled. "Come here," he said.

138

I went to his chair, knelt on the floor, and wedged myself between his legs.

"I don't want you walking down there alone," he whispered, smoothing my hair, the windblown curls. "It's not safe. I was worried about you."

And then I experienced what he'd experienced when he walked through the front door—an empty house, a soundless house. I felt his panic.

"I know," I said. "I should've left a note. I wasn't thinking…" I looked up to see forgiveness, but I couldn't see him clearly enough: the sunset had set our house into shadow.

Later that night, alone in my study, Andy in the living room watching *Match of the Day*, I opened up my little notebook, the one I'd tucked in my windbreaker pocket, and began reading what I'd written—the image-laden lines that had come rushing out during my walk by the sea, lines written to the healing sounds of water.

The name of the teacher that wanted to treat him to a pint was Ronnie O'Brian. This is what Andy told me at the Cultra Inn the following day.

"Give a good tip," said Andy, setting down our fresh pints, "get a good pour of Guinness."

I smiled. I knew to smile.

During our last visit I'd said, "Do you need to tip that much?" This led to another fight and to Andy entering the silence box, a place to which only he held the key. No matter how many times I knocked on that invisible door—*Andy, talk to me*—there was no answer. I had to wait until he chose to come out again.

I was truly alone when that happened. No. More than alone, negative-integer alone, less than zero. *You don't count. You are nothing.* Such relief when he returned.

Is that how Mom felt growing up with Nana?—the deliberate silences, her refusal to speak. I thought some more. Was that why she ended up marrying a man who would hurt her? The ease with which abuse happens—how the horrible becomes normal.

I tried not to worry about money. He always said once his book was published there'd be more opportunities, like writer-in-residence posts.

"You want me to bartend? Is that it?" he'd said one night before turning silent.

"No," I said, feeling sheepish and cornered.

Money can't bring back the dead.

But running a house that needed work given its twenty-year-old state and supporting Mira and the girls—the petrol it took to drive them there and back and there and back, gas wasn't cheap in Northern Ireland—and the bills from the lawyers, the divorce lawyer, and we still had to pay the rest of the bill from the one in Massachusetts, plus Andy's growing expenses like the new computer—it added up.

So Guinness felt good going down my throat at the Cultra Inn.

"Andy!" said the sandy-haired woman the moment we walked through the door of the Cultra Inn the following Friday. Her smile revealed perfect teeth. She was sitting at the table near the jukebox where Andy never sat—he couldn't see the door from there. The man she was sitting beside wore a black leather jacket like Andy's, but his dark hair was peppered with grey and his forehead lined with wrinkles.

They stood up to greet us. We all shook hands and sat down. Names went back and forth.

The barman brought Andy his Guinness. "Same for you today?" he said to me.

I nodded. Ronnie and Ron already had glasses of red wine.

"Cheers," said Andy, lifting his pint.

Ron looked my way and lowered his glass. "Caitlin doesn't have a drink."

"Go ahead," I said.

They watched Andy sip.

"We can wait," said Ronnie. She smiled my way.

I smiled back.

Andy wiped his mouth.

The barman put down my Guinness.

"Now let's toast," said Ron, raising his glass. Ronnie did the same.

"Yous go ahead," said Andy, standing up from the table. He headed to the back, to the men's room.

"He okay?" said Ron, leaning forward.

"He's fine," I said, and sipped my beer to avoid saying more. *I don't think I did anything wrong.*

"Canada," said Ronnie. She tapped Ron's arm, his leather jacket. "We'd love to go there someday."

"But you have here."

"Here?" said Ron, looking around the bar. "This bloody place?" He laughed. "I'm surprised the two of you came back."

"The girls, remember?" said Ronnie. "Ron has kids too."

"And an ex that's…"

I nodded. "We can't blame them though, can we?"

"Do you write?" Ron asked.

"Well…"

"Poetry," said Ronnie.

"Andy told you."

"No, he never said anything about your writing. I saw your poems in *Duelling Words*. Lovely stuff. You're working on more?"

"Right," said Andy, sitting down, cutting the conversation. He looked at the jukebox and then at my purse. "Who's for some music?"

"I like them," I said as I drove us home. With no fog or rain, the dark road was easy to navigate. The night sky was clear except for a sliver of moon. "They should come to Tornley's launch. I'll add their names to the invite list."

"Right."

"Right?" I said, taking the bait.

"A bit too chummy."

"Chummy?"

"She acts like she's your best friend. You hardly know her."

"She was being nice, Andy."

"She practically demanded to see your poems."

"She did? No, she didn't. She just asked when my book was coming out."

"You really could use more journal publications."

"I have two poems coming out, remember?" Two acceptances in a week. Bang. Bang. I'd thumbtacked the evidence to my bulletin board.

"Tornley's Iceland poems are next. We need to man our stable first."

We drove in silence after that. I flicked on the indicator long before our turn: *tick, tick, tick.*

They did come to Tornley's launch and the launch after that. While Andy milled about I could be happy with R & R. I finally had friends I could chat with during literary events, instead of feeling drained by small talk.

The three of us laughed at the posing and put-on airs. There was always someone manoeuvring their way towards Andy to make contact so he'd take a look at their manuscript. I'd see him sizing up the wannabe writer—that practiced look of discernment and friendly pat on the arm.

"So, when is your book coming out?" asked Ronnie. She nibbled on a cube of orange cheese. Even with pumps she barely reached my shoulders. Ron was closer to Andy's height, though he didn't quite match his six-foot-three frame.

Ron nudged my arm. "Come on, tell us."

"Soon. So he says."

"You should get him to commit to a date," said Ronnie.

I didn't answer. They watched me sip my wine.

Ron nudged my elbow. "Maybe he's afraid of how good you are. Ever consider that?"

I shook my head. "He doesn't get rejected like me."

"All writers get rejected, Caitlin," said Ronnie. "Look what happened to Joyce."

"Andy never does."

Ronnie and Ron exchanged glances.

"What?"

"Are you sure about that?" said Ron. "That's not what we've heard."

"What are you talking about?"

"Just stuff, Caitlin," Ronnie said. "It's a small world, you know… Anyway, everyone knows how good a poet Andy is. We bet your book will be just as good."

"If it gets published," I said.

"If? It isn't *if*, missy," Ron said. "It's *when*."

I decided to stop asking about my book. I was tired of asking. I found myself tired more and more often. Afternoon naps—they didn't help. My larval body, like my mind, felt clouded and heavy. The drowning woman came back to me, her bloated body moving through the quarry, the water cradling her pain, her last breath pushing through the white caps, little caps like nurses' caps.

"There you are," he said, entering the girls' bedroom. He tugged at the moon-and-stars duvet. "Anybody in there? You asleep?"

"No," I said, sitting up, knocking Grace's stuffed bear on to the floor. "Tell me, Andy. What colour is love?"

"Pick a shade, any shade." He tossed the bear onto Chel's bed.

"That's it?"

"Why are you fixated on this? Come with me to get the girls, will you? It would be nice to have some company for a change."

I'd done it before—accompanied him back to that place. When he'd pulled the Toyota into Mira's driveway the last time I was with him, he'd parked it at a respectful angle so she wouldn't see me if she happened to be sitting by the living room window or at the kitchen sink doing dishes. Their tug of war had an even weight to it now. This is what I do. This is what you do. No surprises. Did she know I was here illegally? She would've used that threat by now, wouldn't she? Perhaps she did know and it was my money—her continual access to it—that kept me safe.

That last time I went with Andy he made a stop at the corner store on the Island Road. The same moment we drove into the Spar parking lot, Benny and Janet were backing out. Andy glared openly at the man he'd once shared his poems with. He glared and glared until Benny looked away.

I pulled the moon-and-stars duvet up to my chin, closing my cocoon.

"Right," he said.

When he left the room, I put the bear back on Grace's bed.

She must have thought we wouldn't hear her because the living room door was closed. She must've thought the glass door was soundproof.

She was often the first to wake up, to emerge from the moon-and-stars duvet, her little sister asleep in the twin beside hers, the soother lodged in her mouth. Slipping down the stairs, past our closed bedroom door, she must've heard her father snoring. He always snored heavily after a night out at the Cultra Inn, so I had that extra pillow jammed over my head to help block the intermittent rumbling.

Sunday morning cartoons. All to herself. No sister to fight with (yet). The room was hers. She could sprawl on the fireside carpet or on her father's easy chair or she could stretch out on the sofa. But no, this particular morning she didn't want to do any of that. She didn't want to watch silly cartoons. She saw the anthology leaning there—*Duelling Signs*—set it on the easy chair and pulled out the bench from the upright grand. After lifting the piano lid like the coffin it was, she pressed down on the ivory keys. Who had taught her "Chopsticks"? Was every child born knowing that two-fingered song?

Andy slept through it. I couldn't. The sound woke me like a ghost.

I whipped the glass door open. When she turned, she saw my heated face, her finger still pressing middle C. She lifted her finger and the reverberation stopped. She closed the lid and slid the bench back in.

The seaside town of Holywood, the closest town to Craigavad, was only a short train ride away, a ride I hardly took, for whenever I did go into town I always went with Andy. Buildings stood side by side along the bustling street with locals stopping for a "chin-wag." Elderly women dressed in boxy dresses wearing translucent rain bonnets to protect their perms and pin curls and grey-haired men dressed in tweed jackets and matching caps. I'd never seen a Maypole before. It was the only one left in Northern Ireland. I imagined girls in their frilly white dresses on the first of May holding up the long blue ribbons as they circled round and round, never getting dizzy, knowing what to do, clockwise, counter-clockwise, gyrating in planned rotating circles, where to step and when to stop, the centre keeping them fixed in perfect form.

I barely went out of the house now. I had to push through the membrane of strange.

I stepped onto the station platform and waited. What if I run into—no, they live in County Antrim, remember that. The knowers and gossipers. This is County Down.

Lawn mower. Crow. Someone laughing.

The train arrived and I got on.

I thought back to that first train ride to Dublin. The feelings inside so different then. *Alive, alive-oh.* What song played in me now?

No tune came up. Not even a hum.

We'd been living here for how long? I'd lost track. And yet I still felt the outsider. Here and not here. The way light was particle and wave.

I looked out the passenger window. The early morning rain had cleared. Sunshine dewed the leaves into a silvery glisten, like jewels of light.

I walked up Main Street and headed towards the library. Once inside, I tried to shake off the stares from the middle-aged librarians behind the counter—*we know about you.* I avoided their eyes and dropped off my books, walked out of the building and into the sun.

"Caitlin!"

Across the street Geri stood waving. I waved back. She curled her hand: *come over.*

She wasn't wearing a coat and despite the sunshine it was chilly outside. She crossed her arms and turned to the window, to the storefront glass, to the display of used knick-knacks and toys and household items.

"Well," she said, hugging herself. "Did I do a good job? Would it entice you in?"

The assortment, what Andy called "tchotchkes," sat strategically along the windowsill like a choir of lost things. She took hold of my elbow and led me through the glass door.

I'd passed the Oxfam Shop before but I'd never been inside. It smelled of the past but not in a musty way. Donations would not smell musty along the Golden Mile.

A strawberry-blonde woman hanging a red-beaded neck-lace on a headless mannequin turned to Geri. "How's that, Ger?" she said, letting go of the chunky beads.

"Much better. The poor girl's got some colour now."

They both chuckled.

"Sally, I'd like you to meet my neighbour, Caitlin."

"Hiya," said Sally. "Welcome to Oxfam."

"Caitlin's from Canada."

"Lovely! I'd love to go to Canada. See those mountains."

"Oh, I don't live near them."

A woman's voice from the back room called for Sally.

"Excuse me, Caitlin. Coming, Helen!"

"Sally's the Manager," Geri said.

"I didn't know you worked here."

"I don't. I volunteer. Monday afternoons. Been doing it for years." She looked across the room at the wall of food items. "You must try some of their delicious chocolate."

I followed Geri from the rainbow of clothes on circle racks, towards the shelves of stacked food and colourful hand-icrafts—baskets, bowls, drums, and vases.

"Fair Trade," she said, unwrapping a bar. She broke off a square of dark chocolate and handed it to me.

It melted on my tongue. "Delicious."

"Here," she said, handing me the rest. "God knows I don't need it." She touched her cashmere sweater, her flat stomach. "Have a look around. You might see something you like." She headed towards the till. When she stood behind the little counter she said, "Do you need a lift home?"

"I'd love a lift," I said, eyeing the colour red.

I knew what it was to be led through that glass door by Geri. To be surrounded by used things, pretty used things. Misfits made to shine back to the shadow of their former selves in hopes of finding a home. And I knew (deep down I knew) these women, Geri and Sally, like Ron and Ronnie, would become important to me. I could feel it in my bones like comforting nudges or warm tremors, so I held my breath to trap the truth that wanted to come out—*not now, not yet.*

"Cat?" Andy said when he closed the front door.

"In here," I turned from the wall of mirrors. When he entered the master bedroom I smiled back at my reflection. "What do you think?"

"Where would you wear that?"

"I don't know," I said, touching the red silk. "Book launch, maybe?"

"This another hint?"

"No," I said. "I didn't mean that."

He eyed my knees. "It's pretty short."

"It's barely above the knees," I said, tugging the hem, blinking back the sting. "I thought you'd like it."

"It's a cracker of a dress, for Grace when she's older. Where'd you get it?"

"Oxfam. I had library books to return—" *He'll be okay with this, won't he?*

"You're buying second-hand clothes, cast-offs?"

I didn't see it that way, but saying what I thought would only get him going. "It's for charity," I said, trying to reach the back zipper. "I'll be there next week."

"For what?"

"I'm volunteering," I said, still struggling with the zipper. "Geri's there too."

"So she set this up."

"She didn't 'set this up.' Sally, the manager, she's looking for volunteers. They need someone to fill in the Wednesday afternoon shift." The zipper wouldn't go down. "Can you help me with this?"

He unzipped it.

I avoided his face in the mirror. I didn't want to see it closing up, going dark like the inside of a closet.

"You could've told me first. Who else works there, some boy that fancies you?"

"They're older women, Andy. Come on."

"Okay, okay… but remember, I'm going to need help with the press. If it gets in the way…"

"I know," I said. "I'll stop." I checked my watch. "Pizza should be near ready."

"Kiss me," he said.

"What?"

"Come on. Give yer man a kiss."

I kissed him quick on the lips and he pulled me in to kiss him with mouth and tongue and I was in the backseat of a car being kissed by a boy I didn't like, counting the passing headlights across an open field.

"Give me a minute to wash up." He left the room.

I tossed the dress onto the closet floor and changed into my regular clothes—my long denim skirt and baggy mohair sweater.

I looked down at the crumpled red, then picked it up and held it against me. I recalled Sally's words: "You shouldn't hide that lovely figure."

The women who volunteered were much older than I was. Aileen, a busty blonde with curly hair, taught me how to work the till. I took the customer's money and gave back the correct change. "Have a nice day." "Come again." It felt good being part of the community.

We were all volunteers except Sally. She told me this during my break in the back room. We were sitting on pull-out chairs by the tiny pullout table. I wasn't sure what to say when she stopped talking, but she didn't pry. She could sit in the pocket of my silence. She wasn't like the other woman there. The other woman used the fifteen-minute break as a one-way talking session. They had no problem talking freely about themselves. I couldn't imagine doing that.

Sally told me that Geri was one of the few volunteers who'd made it easy for her to take over from the manager she'd been hired to replace.

"They watch me, so they do, the core of them from the old days. Helen, she's the ringleader. I can't tell you how many times I've shown her how to hang clothes on the new hangers." She shook her head. "She deliberately hangs them the old way every time." She took the last puff of her cigarette and butted it out in the ashtray. "Bad habit, I know." She sprayed the air with a can of lilac air freshener. "One day I'll quit. By the way, I meant to ask you, did your hubby like your red dress?"

"He's not my husband… not yet."

"Well," she said, leaning towards me. "Liam, my Liam, we've been together for seven years but we just married this past winter. We went to St. Lucia. My Laura absolutely adores him."

"He's not her father?"

"No—my first husband, he was. Well, sometimes you have to kiss a few frogs before you find your prince." She sighed. "Ach, go on, have a cookie, isn't that what you call them?" She touched the bag of Peek Freans. "I must show you the wedding photos sometime."

Later that day Sally placed the last of the tiny bamboo boxes on top of the pyramid she'd created in the front shop window. "I think they'll sell well, don't you?"

I nodded.

I'd seen them before. Aunt Doris had given me a box, years ago. "Worry dolls," she'd called them. "All the way from Guatemala," she'd said, removing the lid of the box, dropping the contents on her kitchen table. Each doll made a ping on the grey-speckled Formica. Six of the tiniest dolls I'd ever seen. Three boys and three girls. She put one in my hand. I could feel the wire and burlap.

"Tell the doll your worry before going to sleep each night," she said, "then set it by your bedside table and it'll do the worrying for you while you have a good night's sleep. Isn't that a hoot?"

Six dolls, six worries. "What if I have more?" I said, fingering my ponytail.

"More than six? At your age?" She smiled. "That's not possible."

She must've known it was. The biggest worry had surrounded my mother's recent hospital visit for a "woman's operation."

Eventually I learned what the doctors had done—removed her left breast. No way could they hide her red hair falling out.

I thought back to that day I came home from school and found them in the family room—my father sitting in the Windsor chair staring at the carpet, my mother in her chesterfield nook looking out at the quarry, the white caps coming and going, up and down, like endless worries.

"It's cancer, isn't it?"

I'd known all along.

I lifted the top box off the pyramid and headed towards the till to punch in the numbers.

"Oh, no you don't," said Sally, taking hold of my arm. "Let this be my treat. A little thanks for filling in with so many last-minute shifts." She checked her watch. "You're done for the day. Let's go for a coffee at the Maypole, shall we?"

"I… I'd love to, Sally, but, well, Andy will be home soon."

Take one out for every worry. / Let them worry while you sleep. / In her dreams the dolls grow angry—we have worries for you to keep.

I reread the lines that had come rushing onto the page of my notebook the moment I sat down at my desk.

We have worries for you to keep.

Worry dolls didn't want to worry even if worrying took them out of the box. Inside the box they could be together, safe. Outside the box was where the worries happened, worries that weren't your own, that you were forced to take on, a linked chain of handcuffed worries. Tied and strapped with force-fed thoughts: *Think this, doll. My thoughts demand space inside your small mind, those vacant thought bubbles— nothing but air, you are, balloon girl. You need me to anchor you in place.*

The worry dolls reminded me of two other dolls: antique dolls from the turn of the century that belonged to Nana as a little girl. She'd brought them to the quarry as a gift for Mom when she came to live with us. I'd seen the dolls before at Nana's house, in a photo that should've been black and white but was magically coloured. It hung on her living room wall in a gold oval frame. The pretty ribbon-haired girl that was once Nana stared back at the viewer. Her cherub face framed in auburn ringlets, as poised as the porcelain dolls crooked in her arms.

The dolls sat on a shelf in our family room so they could be admired by visitors, neighbours, and the rotating nurses.

"You watch," Dad had whispered when Nana left the family room to change out of her funeral clothes.

"Watch what?" I whispered back.

He pointed to the dolls behind him. "She'll be wanting those."

"But they're Mom's."

"You're damn right they're your mother's. And now they're yours." He shook his head and looked at the floor.

The next morning Nana was gone, back to her red-brick house in Owen Sound. The dolls were gone too.

After the car accident, months after Dad's death, I found them in his study closet hidden behind boxes of envelopes. Their antique eyes clicked open when I set them upright on their imaginary stands in my imaginary room.

I dreamed they moved. I dreamed they had no faces.

And then I gave them back to Nana.

It's cancer, isn't it? The knowing rose out of my mouth, a force all its own—and my parents didn't deny it or say, *Honey, of course it's not cancer*. That piece of conversation never came, only their blue eyes looking up at me as I stood in the family room squeezing my schoolbooks against my chest. I knew then there was more to be afraid of. This knowing inside me had a life.

We were sitting on the dock watching the sunset over the quarry. One of the many things we did after Mom died. I always felt her presence during those moments, as if the air was her breath through the glow. But that evening I didn't feel her breath. What I felt was an ache, a constriction that began at the base of the neck and ended deep in my stomach.

He was drinking beer and wanted to talk. He'd taken a big risk leaving his old envelope company to work for the competition because of his age, but he'd brought his key clients with him. Even I knew you weren't supposed to do that. Yet somehow he'd done it. He was good at doing things he shouldn't do. At making things happen. And what he said next deepened the constriction.

"I've made a will."

"Dad?"

"You heard me. You need to know." He squeezed my knee like he did when I wore pigtails and looked up to him like a god.

I took a deep breath and said, *There's this knowing inside me that signals things. It begins as sensation, a ripple of constriction, and after settling in my stomach, it travels into my mind, into image, and it's given me an image of you in danger—you in your car, your Caddy. It's happened before. It happened with Mom. Remember that day in the family room when I knew she had cancer? And later how I knew she'd die Christmas Day? That image practically screamed at me, so when you came home from the hospital and said,* she's gone, *and I said,* I know, *I did know, see? So will you please stay home tonight? Don't go to Buffalo. We can order pizza and watch 20/20... what do you say?*

If I'd said that he'd be alive.

Right now.

Right.

Now.

There was no will. He'd lied about the will.

I began to define a good day by negatives: I didn't receive a rejection slip, I didn't dream of Mira, I didn't set him off to the dark place, I didn't talk about my parents to set him off to the dark place, I didn't wear the wrong thing, I didn't eat an apple in front of him (how he hates the sound of my crunching jaw, he can't even look at me).

When did that start? In Dublin we ate them together, sitting on a park bench in St. Stephen's Green, apples purchased from the nearby Spar. Eating an apple required crunch—bite through skin.

I was snuggled under the moon-and-stars duvet and almost asleep when I heard his footsteps climbing the stairs.

"I got it. Look!" He whipped the duvet off my fetal body.

I sat up and took hold of the letter. I'd forgotten about his application for the writer-in-residence post. "Amherst University... It says you can bring a spouse—"

"Cat, hon." He sat down, tilting the mattress. I shimmied over.

"It's only a three-week post. Besides… your passport, remember?"

"Three weeks? It's a month, Andy. We've never been apart for a month."

"I'll miss you, you know that, but this—" He grabbed the paper from my hand. "A ticket to new opportunities."

"Amherst," I said. I thought of the Dickinson homestead. *What if he runs into that blonde tour guide?*

He tapped my knee. "And to think you wanted to high-tail us out of there, remember? I would've been barred from going back." He looked at the letter. "We would've missed this."

The weight on the single bed lifted.

"Where are you going?"

"I'm calling Patrick. Hemming and hawing about coming up tonight, says he's tired. He needs to come up. We've got plans to make with my trip to America."

"I'd like to come too, Andy. You'll be celebrating."

He stopped at the door and turned back. I couldn't remember the last time I'd seen him so happy.

It gets blurry now. In the middle of what happens, when the blindness of love has removed the dark cloak. I started to see what I didn't want to see, so I worked harder at not seeing, at being blind. Running helped; self-induced endorphins triggered my quarried heart.

Just to be near him, in a car, in a pub, was to feel *alive, alive, oh*. Where had that gone?

In Ontario leaves burn out their final colours, red and gold through the shivering months. In Northern Ireland they barely turn yellow. Leaves trapped in light.

I was thinking this while looking out my study window. I was trying not to listen to his firm voice through the wall.

"Cat," Andy said after the click of the phone. "You there?"

I stood up from my chair and entered his study.

"Go on," he said. "Have a seat."

I sat down on the wooden chair. "How'd she take it?"

"She's not happy about having to drive them while I'm gone. She'll see how much I put into it, going back and forth."

"Drive them?"

"I think she's jealous. Nobody's asking her to come to America."

"I won't be taking the girls while you're gone, Andy."

"What do you mean *won't*?"

"We have them every weekend. And who looks after them when you're out?"

"Ah, so that's it. Can't make it easy for me."

"I won't feel right having them here without you. Mira, the girls, they'll just have to understand." *I'll miss them, yes, but I should get a break too.* "Like you said, it's not that long."

"You don't want them. Come out and say it."

"You think other women would do what I've done? Pay for this. Pay for that."

"Is this what the Oxfam brigade's telling you? Right. Shove the money thing in my face. All about money, you and—"

"Don't you dare say her name."

"What are you going to do? Party with your new buddies? Have a threesome with the *Two Ronnies*?"

I refused to laugh. He loved watching reruns of that comedy sketch show. I didn't. I folded my arms and stood up.

"Go on, do your own thing." He stood up from his chair and headed for the door, but then turned to stand in front of me. "If I find out you've been seeing Tornley or that Greek guy who's been coming to the launches."

"Nikos?"

"I saw him chatting you up."

"He's Ron and Ronnie's friend. He has nothing to do with me."

"You watch."

"God, Andy."

"Mark my words." He wagged his finger in my face.

This time I did laugh. His cartoon act—where was it coming from?

"You think it's funny?" He twisted my arm and I stopped laughing.

"Stop it," I said, and pulled away.

He smiled and out came a chuckle.

Kenny from Rathcoole supplied it in dark chestnut chunks. Smoking up. What we did when we didn't want to go out but still wanted to celebrate—another review of his book, another complimentary letter from a fellow writer, another article about the up-and-coming press or more details about his forthcoming visit to America. "We" were making impact here in Craigavad.

I knew all the stages of birthing a book now. From acquiring the ISBN to final boxed production. I'd helped with packing up review copies, mailing launch invites. I even proofread.

"My little 'poof' reader," Andy said, pointing to the word in question. "It's *piece* not *peace*."

I followed his index finger.

"Piece." And I thought of falling snow.

"Andy," I said, looking down the store aisle.

We turned from the shelves of light bulbs towards the display of model kitchens.

Andy read the massive sign, the special they were offering. "We could do this," he said, squeezing my hand.

"You think so?"

"The money I'm bringing in? The divorce on the horizon?" He eyed the red kitchen. "This would look great in our house."

Our house. It was good to hear him say that. Instead of: *What if something happens to you, Cat? I'll have nowhere to go. I'll be homeless.* When I finally understood the source of his fears, what must've led to his moods and nightmares, I saw how vulnerable he really was. Since I'd made out a will naming Andy as beneficiary, we were no longer fighting.

"I know," I said, touching a glossy cupboard. I thought back to Aunt Doris's comment. Red is fun for kitchens.

"You deserve it, Pet."

"I don't know—"

"Come on. Let's talk to the salesman."

That night, while smoking up in the kitchen, we imagined the red wrapped around us. We were good at that, imagining, seeing the colour that wasn't there.

I was in the high-risk category with a mother who'd died from breast cancer early in life, so I was supposed to check for lumps after each period. But my cycle, normally regular, had disappeared since living in Craigavad, and other symptoms had heightened—tender breasts and sensitive nipples. The thought of his touch created a flinch of pain. "Not now, Andy." This comment had increased in frequency along with emotional outbursts, tears that came suddenly, unbidden. And I was tired, so tired, from not sleeping through his loud snoring, so we agreed I should sleep in Grace's bed during the week.

Chel's curls had finally outgrown the tight spirals that so frustrated her. Her hair was long enough to sport a ponytail. Yet now that she could wear one, she never did. She left her hair wild and loose. One Saturday afternoon she found me alone in my study—a deck of cards in her small chubby hands.

"Later, Chel," I said. "Okay?"

She didn't move. She just stood there looking at me with the eyes of her mother.

Pushing the door wide open, she headed to the shelf where I'd placed the worry dolls. She reached for the bamboo box.

"No!"

She jumped back.

I'd scared her but I didn't alter my tone. "They're not for touching, Rachel." I flinched. I sounded like Nana.

She stood there twisting her fingers, and shouted, "Mummy says dolls are for play." Then she marched out of the room.

Dolls are for play. That night while lying in bed I was thinking these words when I felt the lump. Marble hard. The size of a pea. I sat up, Andy put down his book.

After flattening them one at a time on cold metal plates the technician guided me to a grey-lit room where she jellied the breast in question then ran a smooth cold wand over the glossed-slick skin while viewing the grainy waves of black and white on the small screen. Subterranean tissue, there, transformed. I could see the culprit—the fibrous knot.

Andy was sitting in the waiting room when I told him what the technician had told me, though she'd said nothing at first. "The doctor will have to diagnose this," she said when I asked for the results. But when she saw the worry—so palpable on my face, she could probably smell it—she whispered in my ear, "*Fibroadenoma.* Quite common in dense breasts. You're safe, luv." And the six worry dolls roaming inside me slipped back into their bamboo box.

No, five. Part of me was disappointed. Part of me wanted to be sick.

I pressed my nose into his maroon cotton T-shirt, the one he slept in, the one he hadn't taken to America, to take in his masculine scent, then went from room to room straightening and cleaning. I should've put on music but I wanted to hear the silence, be inside it. But his voice came through—*You're obsessed with cleaning like your Nana.*

Dark clouds on the horizon countered the sunlight as I stood in the shiny red kitchen. I looked out at the back of our house, at the hill of lawn that led to the hedge of the upper garden. There was always something blooming there, giving colour—roses, holly, gorse.

And then the rain came down nail straight, the perfect veil. Not a hint of slant in the falling. I wanted to see what it looked like over the Lough, so I walked out of the kitchen into the living room, but when I looked outside I saw no rain. Nothing fell. And when I stepped out the front door only the air touched me. I ran to the back and out the back door, where rain pinned me down.

I got into a new rhythm. Went to bed early, woke up early, ate less, drank less, didn't smoke up, started writing poems, doll poems. I was too close to judge them objectively so I tucked them aside to give time for fresh eyes. I'd even started wearing fashionable clothes again—jeans with trendy tops I'd purchased at Oxfam—instead of the usual sweatshirt and track pants. One day, having bathed and dressed in an outfit I used to wear when teaching—a pencil skirt and silk blouse—I stepped out to walk around the house and then re-entered through the back door, straight to my study, as if going to work.

It felt good living in the imagination again, my outer life feeding my inner life and vice versa. It brought back memories of the red-door cottage, of drinking tea while listening to the lulling waves of the sea, the incoming foam crisping and nudging the pebbles to sound. Though I had a view here, a stunning sea view, the waves were distant and mute.

He called every day. It was good to hear his voice. He sounded happy. That part I didn't like. *Don't you miss me?*

How can you be happy with me not there? The daily conversations were nothing like the ones we'd had when I'd called from the red phone box. *Ring one, hang up, count to ten, ring again.* The thrill they'd spark inside.

"Did you hear that, Cat? The key to the city. Can you believe it? A bloke from Rathcoole."

"That's great, Andy."

He sighed. "You don't sound like it's great. Don't tell me you're going to go all Mira on me."

"God, Andy. How can you say that?"

"I knew it."

"You knew?"

"I knew you wouldn't be happy for me. That's why I told Natalie I didn't want to tell you."

"Natalie?"

"I told you about Natalie."

"No, you didn't… Is she a colleague?"

"She's in charge of theatre here. She wants to write a play using my Islandmagee poems."

"Oh."

"Told you this would open up doors for us. I showed her some of your poems too. She really likes them."

"You showed her my poems?"

"You gonna attack me on that now? Go ahead, throw another wobbler, you're good at that."

I stared out the window, the yellow leaves blurred to a haze.

"Right. So it's the silent treatment then. You learned that well from your nana."

"Stop it, Andy."

"You don't want to talk. Let's leave it at that."

"Fine," I said, and put down the phone.

That night when the phone rang I wasn't home. I was out walking by the sea with my little notebook, capturing the words coming to me, trying to ignore the noxious aftertaste from that last phone call. Even with Andy so far away I still had to shake this sensation he was somehow watching me. He told me to not walk the sea trail alone. He made me promise. I thought of my father. "I have my spies out, remember." Spies in the shimmer of the storefront glass, in the cracks of the Grimsby sidewalks, in the leaves of the maple trees. Best to obey, to do what you're told.

But the pull of the sea was too great.

Flushed from the cool salty air and from the excitement of seeing another seal, I sat at Andy's desk and pressed *play* on the answering machine.

But it was Ronnie's cheerful voice that sounded through the room, along with a friendly shout from Ron in the background. Their good friend Nikos was having a house party. They wanted me to come.

I took a taxi to the party. I didn't want to wait for the train in the wet weather wearing the red silk dress. I shook out my umbrella and rang the doorbell. *You can do this. You have to do this.*

Nikos opened the door. His trim beard suited his face but it didn't suit me. It did nothing for me. He extended his hand. I gave him mine.

With the party in full flow, I found a private alcove. *How sad,* I thought, looking out the dark window, *that this is my act of defiance—attending a house party with friends.*

Later that night Nikos passed me a book. "I want you to sign this." *Duelling Words,* held open to the pages with my poems.

I crossed a line through my name and signed below, what real authors do.

"Read them, Caitlin, will you?" said Ronnie.

"Go on," said Ron.

The four of us were the only ones left.

"You sure?"

They sat down on chairs scattered around the room.

I read, and when I finished, the sound of clapping cut the spell I'd cast and for the first time I understood its function. How it breaks the illusion, not just for the audience but for the performer as well.

Nana and I are watching a bearded man chewing something. She puts her arm around me. I am shocked by her touch.

"Spit it out," she says to the bearded man.

"I have nothing to spit out." He continues chewing.

She stares hard with her saucer-blue eyes. "Now."

He stares back and stops chewing, cups his hand and spits—pink, glistening, wet.

She turns to me and smiles. "See?" And then to him, "Enough!"

She floats away.

She is gone when I wake up.

The phone call came that morning. I thought it would be Andy, but a woman with a Canadian accent spoke through the receiver. She said Nana died peacefully in her sleep, at home like she wanted.

"When?" I said through my dry throat.

"Last night."

"What time?"

"Does it matter? Ten. Yes, ten o'clock."

I did the time change in my head when I awoke from that dream. They matched.

"It's not easy losing a loved one, but your grandmother, she lived a long life. She was a fighter, Florence, but in the end, her heart gave out."

I stared at Andy's pencil, the little chews.

"Caitlin, are you there?"

"I'm there," I said. "I'm here."

Her name, along with her birthdate and dash, had been chiselled on the Maharg family stone at the time of her husband's death, the dash like an open gate, waiting on a date to close. It now had that date.

I couldn't go to the funeral if I wanted to.

I wanted to.

I thought of phoning Ronnie or Geri or Sally. I needed to talk to somebody who cared about me, but I didn't want to clog the phone line. I wanted to be here when he called. He promised he would.

I waited into the night. The phone didn't ring.

"Pet, you answered quick."

I set down my afternoon cup of tea and swivelled in his study chair. The lack of sleep made me shiver.

"Cat? You there?"

"I'm here."

"Your voice sounds funny."

"You didn't call last night."

"I didn't? No. You're right, I didn't. What a night. They took me out after my reading. The lineup for signing books— we ran out of books." He paused. "Cat?"

"My nana died."

"The mean one?"

"She died yesterday."

"Old age?"

"I said *yesterday.*"

"Oh, I get it. So it's my fault your nana died yesterday, is that it? I should've known somehow."

I didn't answer.

"I'm not playing your game."

I still didn't answer.

"If you don't want to talk." His voice softened. "If it's too painful right now…"

"What am I doing with you?"

"What?"

"You heard me."

"Now, calm down. Clearly you're stressed with your nana dying."

"We don't have anything, Andy. Nothing. We have nothing."

"Nothing? You kidding me? You've been alone too long."

"No," I said. I couldn't think. I could only see—pink, glistening, wet.

"Great. My ride's at the door. Can we talk more later?"

"It's Natalie, isn't it." I held my breath. *Answer me.*

He didn't answer.

I hung up the phone.

That night while lying in bed, eyes open to the dark, I thought of water. How it repels off some things and is absorbed by others. How it rises from its source and seeps into cracks. How some never feel guilt. How others feel nothing but.

I stood waiting for arrivals by the sliding glass doors and he came striding in. What I saw in his eyes when he saw mine confirmed the cavern of space between us. We hugged but we didn't kiss.

His scent had changed. A sharper musk.

"The car's just outside," I said.

Did he sleep on the plane? He told me he'd dozed but it was hard to fall asleep with so many thoughts racing through him.

"What a time," he said when he slipped into the passenger seat.

He was reliving the journey… perhaps reliving one moment with one person.

"I want to hear all about it," I said, lying. Or was I? Maybe I did want to know.

He reclined the passenger seat and closed his eyes.

Only when I stopped and pulled the key from the ignition did he open them.

"Are you hungry? Cheese toastie?"

"Hamburger. That's what I feel like. A quarter pounder."

We were ready to step out of the car but Andy just sat there.

"They want me back. I need to sort dates."

"Really?" I said, gripping the steering wheel.

His sleepy eyes widened when he looked my way. "Thanks… I thought…" He unbuckled his seat belt and stepped into the open air, stretched his arms to the morning sky. "Martello Park, Craigavad," he said, as if seeing it for the first time.

Andy started talking about the Internet. Suddenly he had to have it, was so anxious about getting it. The need to receive messages through *e-mail*.

"It's how they do things overseas," Andy said. "The new technology."

"Well, you must have it then."

The night we went out for pints at the Cultra Inn, he told me again how they loved him in America. They'd kept him busy, so he'd earned his keep. "It was magic, Cat." He kept on saying this.

I ignored the twinges in my belly.

Barry Brandon, a professor of Irish Literature at Amherst University, had taken Andy under his wing. He introduced him to the moneyed Americans crazy for the Irish. The wives cooed in adoration, but Andy knew when to pull back. That tightrope balance of having women want him and men want to be him—hadn't he always lived with that? Barry thanked him for not sleeping with his students. Apparently that hadn't happened with the other visiting male poets.

With enough Guinness in him, I slipped in a question.

He smiled. "She was a big help. She was there when Barry wasn't. You should see what she's doing with the poems—transforming them for the stage." His face, full of light the way it used to be during those early days. Brown's Bay. Dublin.

After paying the bar tab we stepped into the cold night air. Familiar lyrics rose from a car parked parallel to ours. "On Raglan Road."

"Andy."

"Yeah?"

The voice of Van Morrison stopped when the engine started. *Keep your eye on the ball.* "Nothing."

The girls dropped their plastic bags on the front hall carpet. "It's like Christmas!" Grace said. "Where are they, Dad? Can we open them now?"

Chel nodded. "Can we, Da?"

"Hold on," Andy said. "We've got all night."

"That trip took longer than usual," I said, walking towards them from my study.

"Ran into Kenny on the way," he said, winking. He patted his jeans pocket where the lump of hash should be, but his pocket was flat.

Ring once, hang up, count to ten, ring again.

"Daaa," said Grace, tugging the sleeve of his leather jacket. "Take off your coat."

Chel grabbed for the lower sleeve. "Yeah, Daaa. We want prezzies."

"Hold on, will ya," he said, pulling away. "You'll rip my jacket." He looked at me standing there, watching him. "Aren't you going to say hello to Cat?"

"HiCat," they said as one word.

Grace was starting to turn into the woman she'd be one day. Chel's face had changed too; her round cheeks had thinned. They'd both grown taller. I felt it in their hugs.

"Okay, okay, I'll get the goods. Go on yous two. Go wait in the living room."

The peat fire I'd started was emitting heat and light. The long dark. The price you pay for the light-stretched days of summer.

He brought in two bulky bags. "Sit over there," he said, pointing to the sofa.

Side by side they sat with their knees locked and hands clasped on their laps. He gave them the bags at the very same time.

"Look! Look!" they shouted. Glittery bracelets, shiny necklaces, candy-floss lip gloss. They eyed their goods then eyed each other's. *Did you get what I got? Is what you got better?*

"There's more in there," Andy said.

They dug their hands through the crinkly layers of tissue paper and pulled out boxes. Inside each was a collection of clips in pastel colours shaped like butterflies.

"Natalie says they're the latest thing," Andy said. "What all the cool girls are wearing in America."

"Cool!" said Grace.

"Cool!" said Chel.

Theatre Natalie. Handpicked by Natalie.

Grace uncurled a strand of her little sister's hair and clipped one in. Chel felt for the purple clip. "I want to see!" she shouted. She raced out of the living room, into our bedroom, to the wall of mirrors. Her big sister followed.

We were alone again. I turned to Andy.

He hadn't brought me back any presents. The writer-in-residence post had supplied food, accommodation and various perks, plus modest salary, so we agreed he shouldn't spend more than was necessary.

Had they gone together to buy them? Or did she pick them out on her own? My mind stirred with questions. He avoided my eyes.

Chel raced back into the living room. "Look, Da!" she said, putting her hands on her head to touch what she couldn't see.

"Stop hiding them, Pet."

She put her hands down. Clips of every colour.

Grace entered the room smiling. "They're cool, Dad. Don't they look cool, Cat? Come on, Chel, I want to try something."

Chel danced a little leap. "Okay!" she said, and squealed after her big sister.

They were usually fighting by now. Grace wanting space from Chel. Chel wanting Grace's attention. For a change, a happy moment for this blended family.

Natalie.

I got used to the sound that happened whenever Andy unplugged our phone line to access the internet. *Click.* I heard it in my study with the door closed. *Click.* I heard it in the living room with the television on. *Click.* I heard it in my nightmares. But whenever I knocked at his study door, the game Solitaire shone on his computer screen.

He was addicted to the game (so he said). He was determined to beat his dealt hand.

I was watching television, absorbed in the comedic drama of a show he refused to watch, when he grabbed the remote from my lap and the screen turned dark.

"I was watching that—"

"Did you go to his house party? Did you?"

And then I knew what he knew, the message I'd forgotten to delete on the answering machine. I caught up to his fury.

"No. I didn't go. I worked on poems, okay. Satisfied?"

He stood there watching me. I stood up to watch him.

"Go ahead, call Ron and Ronnie. They know I wasn't there."

"Yeah, right," he said. "You expect me to believe the Two Ronnies?"

"It's me you should believe. I didn't go. I'd never lie to you, Andy."

He blinked and the fierceness in his face—the knitting brows and jutting chin—loosened slightly. "I know, Pet. I don't know what's gotten into me." He tossed the remote back on the chair and returned to his study.

I took hold of the remote and turned the TV back on.

We define ourselves by what we're not; the differences to determine who we are. Prod or Catholic. In love / out of love. Yet when we're inside a cloud we can't see what state we're in. All we know, or hope for, is that we're moving forward.

Days Andy entered his study I went out with my circle of friends. Coffee with Sally after her Oxfam shift, drinks with Ron and Ronnie, afternoon tea with Geri and William. He didn't notice my new absence, absorbed as he was in his upcoming plans, his trip back to America. And then he announced, "I need to go to the Lake District."

A taxi took him to the ferry. It was too risky for me to drive that distance without a license. The days before his departure were a blur—*he won't go without me*—but he did go. "He should want to be with you," Sally had said during my last Oxfam shift. "He hasn't been back that long from America."

There was no telephone in Barry Brandon's Lake District cottage, so it was impossible for me to phone. He would have to phone me from the nearest phone box. They were going to work on an upcoming book, an anthology of Irish art and poetry.

That night when the phone rang, I didn't want to talk. I let it go to message: "It's beautiful here, Cat. One day you'll see. Night, Pet."

Pet. Shake-a-paw. Heel. Sit.

"You're doing the right thing." Sally put her arm around my shoulder.

I rang our neighbour's doorbell. "Am I?"

"I really think Geri can help."

The pamphlet from the Women's Centre was in my purse but the contents were still circulating through my mind. Sally had been advising me to go for weeks; finally her message got through. What made me walk in there this morning on my own, I couldn't say, but I'd felt the pull. Yes, he'd grabbed me by the arm several times now, but he never hit me. Abusers hit. Isn't that what happened to Mom in her first marriage? *He beat her on her wedding night and night after night with his leather belt. He inserted sharp things.*

"Can I help you?" the women had said sitting behind the desk. She put down her pen and smiled.

I shook my head. "Just here for a friend."

"Take your time then. Feel free to take any pamphlets. Your friend is welcome here, too."

I read the stencilled words rimming the wall: *We believe each woman who walks through our door is important and unique. We believe all women should have access to support. Secure. Non-judgmental. Caring.*

I don't belong here. I turned to the door. But when I saw the checklist hanging there—Signs for Emotional Abuse—and started reading it: *undermines decisions, criticizes appearance,*

*isolates you from friends and family, controls your money, is jeal-
ous and possessive, blames you for everything that goes wrong,
demonstrates "omnipotence," induces debility and exhaustion…*
I stood, a deer in headlights, a cage of light.

Everybody knew. Everybody saw this but me.

He was as close to me as Dad was. And when Dad died—I
remember this now—one of the thoughts that entered my
head was: *who will care if I come home again?*

Geri opened the door. "I'm so glad you called. Come in,
please."

I sat down on the sofa I'd sat on before, the one with the
flowery pattern. I didn't look at the chair where he once sat. I
was afraid to see him there, watching this.

"May I get you ladies a drink?"

"Water would be lovely," Sally said.

I nodded.

I wanted to burrow away like a rabbit in a hole, become
a baby rabbit like those pink squirms embedded in the nest
Dad found on our lawn in Grimsby. Squirms with lid-trapped
eyes, there on our lawn. Is that right? Is that what I remember?

"Here you go, Caitlin."

I needed both hands to hold the glass, to stop it from
shaking. The cold streamed down my throat.

You've been taken, Caitlin. Pink, glistening, wet.

One more woman in the room and I'd be back at the Petty
farm listening to three women I refused to listen to.

You think you're the first?

This time I listened.

I needed a new passport. I needed to gain my power back
without him knowing. But I wanted to stay here. I needed
Andy to marry me to stay here.

"May I speak to William about this?" said Geri. "He has
connections."

I nodded.

"My dear girl. Why, I can't say I'm too surprised. You were always in that house looking after him or the girls while he swaggered about. And where's your book? Promises and more promises. Oh, and the money, your parents' money—"

She saw my face. She knew to stop.

In bed that night I thought back to that art teacher who'd turned my B into an A. She'd also taught Phys-Ed. As hard as I tried, as many times as I tried, I could never hold my legs in balance to perform a tripod. I always toppled over.

One day I showed Mom. "See? It's impossible," I said after another unsuccessful attempt. "I'm going to fail."

She put down her cigarette and crouched on the family room floor, the cancer not crippling her body yet, and performed the perfect tripod.

"See how my hands and head form a triangle?" Mom said. "You need a strong base to keep the legs in balance. Try it, honey."

I positioned my head on the pillow she'd set there and made a triangle with my head and my hands, then pushed my feet up off the ground and set my knees on my arms. It was that easy.

When Andy returned from the Lake District I could smell her scent on his skin. Even after he bathed I could smell it, as if she lived inside him like I once did: *You're inside me, Cat.*

"This book will be brilliant," Andy said, holding a fresh cup of tea. "Barry and I made good headway. It'll put the Mourne Press on the map." He grinned. "But then we're already on the map." He watched me lace my running shoes. "How long will you be?"

"Oh, a while. Close to an hour," I said, lying.

"Stay safe, Pet. Don't go down to the sea."

Ten minutes later I came back as planned and opened the front door as quietly as possible. I was good at being quiet. As

I headed to his study I could tell from the tone of his voice he was talking to someone he knew well.

I opened the door and yanked the receiver from his hand. "Hello?" I shouted into the mouthpiece.

He grabbed it back. "What the fuck do you think you're doing?"

"Who's that? Who are you talking to?"

He held the receiver high in the air, I couldn't reach it. I ran out of the room to lift the one in the bedroom—I should've gone there first—but he caught up to me and gripped my arm.

"Stop it! You're hurting me!" Somehow I squirmed out of his hold and raced into the bathroom, slammed the door in time to lock it, my heart beating like a trapped animal. I crouched on the cold tile floor, hugged my knees to my chest.

He pounded the door. He shouted, "Open up! Now!"

I flinched.

And then all went quiet.

I heard *click* down the hall. I heard dialling.

The floor tiles were embedded with black wavy lines. No two were the same. They were squirming like worms, writhing. I blinked to stop them from moving.

I rubbed my arm, the vivid redness.

The door handle moved, back and forth.

I shuddered.

"Are you coming out or what?"

Shadows shifted along the bottom of the door as he paced.

"Fine. Stay there all night then."

"Here, Pet. I made you some tea."

I pushed the moon-and-stars duvet off my chest, sat up and leaned back against the headboard, my mind still full of the nightmare. This time when Mom's beckoning hand appeared from the open coffin I had looked deep inside to see the damage her abuser had done—a hole in her white wedding dress where her heart had been. Quarried. Nothing but wood beneath it.

The way death comes back to you, the shock—that's how last night came rushing in. I hugged my knees for comfort like I did on the bathroom floor.

He took my move as a sign to sit down at the edge of Grace's bed.

The mug of tea sat lukewarm in my hands.

"That book I'm working on with Barry that celebrates Irish art." He smiled, his cheeks the shade of ripe apples. "I want *you* to be one of the poets."

"Me?"

"Look. There's a lot going on in my head right now," he said. "You'll need to pick a painting for your poem soon." He tapped my knee. Then, "You're not drinking your tea."

I sipped.

"There's so much to organize before my trip back. I could sure use your help."

"When haven't I helped you, Andy?"

"I know, I know."

Ask him now. "Have you set your departure date yet?"

"Soon. They're sorting out the funding."

No mention of last night. As if nothing happened.

He left the room.

Apple. Apple cheeks. Apple.

He hated my mouth on the flesh of an apple. He couldn't stand the apple sound or the apple sight of my apple chew. He even blocked me with his hand or swivelled his chair to another angle.

The tea had too much milk in it. He'd made it the way he liked it.

"It's that easy?" I said, looking at the passport form I had to fill in. I felt like a fool sitting at William and Geri's kitchen table.

They both nodded.

I fingered the blocks of blank spaces. "I'll have to go back now."

Geri touched my arm. "You're still a young woman, sweetie. You'll build a new life in Canada. It's home."

When I finished filling it out, I handed it back to Geri. She left the kitchen.

William smiled at my puzzled face. "Not to worry, she'll be right back."

A moment later Geri returned with the big blue vase from the living room. She raised it up like a trophy, like Mom's trophy with the tiny gold woman holding a racquet mid-serve. "The day your passport arrives, we'll put this in the front window. Watch for it on your runs."

I thought back to Mira, how her passivity became her power—she was preparing herself for the perfect moment, the beginning of the end, when she would slam it in his jet-lagged face. And ask for the money. And more money. I understood her now.

But would I have my perfect moment? *What if the new passport doesn't arrive in time and I lose my chance while he's gone?* Bar him from the house when he gets back from overseas like Mira and he'll call the authorities and have me deported. But no, he wouldn't do that. Obtaining a new passport was only part of the journey. There were other things I needed to do, to protect myself: change the will, sell the house, find an overseas mover… but I didn't want to leave.

The thought of dismantling my dream, piece by piece, felt overwhelming, like grief. *How much longer can I go on like this?* The urge to burrow beneath the moon-and-stars duvet. To leave the world in sleep.

I took the train down to Oxfam to see Sally. She was dressing the headless mannequin, knotting a green scarf around her neck when I came in.

At the Maypole Café, when we went to chat, I slipped off my coat and the sleeve of my sweater slid up.

She eyed the mark on my arm. "Caitlin?"

I pulled down the sleeve. "He has to marry me. How else will I stay here?"

She shook her head.

"He promised me, Sally. Maybe there is no Natalie. Maybe it's all in my head—"

"Natalie or not, it's over, honey." She patted my knee. "Your father, from what you've told me, he was overprotective, sure, but that came from love. Men like Andy, like my ex, I call them 'Oz-boys.' Pull back the curtain and what do we see? A titch of a man, a nothing. Men, no, boys like Andy, all they do is slabber—they're hollow inside. It's about control. They can't face their own pain, their feelings of failure so they seek the light in others. In a strange way, if this makes any sense, think of it, well, he saw the light that is you."

Dear Mom,

There is nowhere for me to go. What I believed is gone. How to rebuild? He was my foundation. I have no foundation. What did you do when you hit rock bottom? Marriage is for life. Till death do us part. *But you were dying a living death with the man before Dad. You became a shell of your former self. Like me. I've seen your quarried heart. He hasn't taken all of mine from me, has he? The heart of me that is you.*

I saw how you battled with cancer; you never gave up— through the surgery, radiation, the chemo, the bone-pain, the declining eyesight, there you were, under the living room lamp- light, creating works with your hands. A thread through the needle's eye, determination pulling you through the pain. You went on after the abuse of that first marriage. You lived a new life with Dad.

For me to give up now—no. It would dishonour you.

He came rushing out of his study when I returned from my run. Vibrating with enthusiasm, he couldn't hold his news. He had to tell someone even if that someone was me. He'd just set his return date to America.

"That's great," I said. And it was. Fly to Canada and back before Andy got back, he would have nothing over me then.

"I picked a painting for your book," I said, untying my shoes.

"And?"

"Jack B. Yeats."

"Which one?"

The black pit of depression. The horse of white hope.

"*Grief.*"

Cast a cold eye on life, on death. Horseman, pass by.

He kissed me softly on the forehead and it woke me up. "I'll miss you," he whispered. "But a month's not that long. Next time I want you to come. You'll come with me, won't you?"

"Of course," I said, opening my eyes, sitting up on Grace's bed.

The click of his brogues down the landing steps, the leaving motor of the taxi, and I was alone in the house again.

After making a cup of tea I sat on his easy chair with my legs curled up and looked out the living room window. The Lough shivered electric blue beneath the penetrating sun; the clouds moved as slowly as the boats beneath.

The perfect image of the perfect day.

Let me make it up to you.

We'd had a lovely time last night.

"I'm taking you out," he'd said. "My treat. Wear that red dress, will you. I want to take that image to Amherst with me."

"You do?"

"I've been distracted lately, I know I have."

After driving us to our destination he'd guided me through the grand doors of the Culloden Hotel—past the ornate lobby, the lobby pay phone, the cushy wing-back chairs, the signed rubber ducks in the glass cabinet, into the five-star restaurant towards a table in the candlelit corner. Linen. Silver. Crystal glasses. Soft music.

"Order anything," he said, topping up my wine.

And we were back in Dublin, back to Raglan Road, back to us.

"I've missed this, Andy." I wiped my eyes. *What you miss is an illusion.*

"Don't cry, Cat. I have a surprise. When I get back from my trip we're doing your book."

"No…"

"What do you mean *no*? We were always going to do your book."

"There's no one else."

"What?"

"No one named Natalie."

"She isn't going to be there."

"I thought she was doing your poems in a play."

"That got scuppered," he said. "She was all talk." He reached for my hand and my hand disappeared.

I sipped more wine. "That a girl," he said, refilling my glass.

It felt good forgetting. I wanted to forget.

When we got back home we sat on the sofa smoking the little brown pipe. He rested his hand on my thigh and moved it higher…

Gazing out at the sea, I set my tea on the table and watched the SeaCat heading to Scotland. With the divorce soon to be final we'd be free to marry. We'd talked about Gretna Green, the Scottish village famous for runaway weddings, just two witnesses and a hammer-banging blacksmith as anvil priest.

We could elope like my parents did—well, like they'd claimed to have done. We could be on the boat I longingly watched from the living room window. Feel the spray from the risen wake. See land meld to water, water rise to land.

I finished my tea and went into his study.

Even in the silence I could hear his voice. I sat in his chair and waited for his computer to boot up. My heartbeat quickened as the screen came to life.

I took a deep breath. I checked the Inbox and then the Outbox. No emails from someone named Natalie. Nothing. Besides, would he have made love to me last night? My breathing slowed with relief.

And there, sitting in something called "Deleted Items" as if waiting for me, an e-mail he must've thought he'd deleted.

Pet,

Where are you, my love? Are you okay? I'm lonely! Please email me now. Will phone today / this evening. Remember: ring one, hang up count to ten, ring again.

Keep going for the prize of you and me. I love you more than life. Tread softly because you tread on my dreams.

I read it sitting down. I read it standing up even though I felt queasy. I walked down the hallway in a thickening daze— *no, no, no*—and the sickness grew. *The thought of his body in mine.* No… no… *no….*

I cupped my hands and out the vomit came—pink, glistening, wet.

Let your bones become the bones of birds, a pathway for air— escape—a tunnel for wings to fly through.

V

Updated passport. *Check.* Change of locks. *Check.* House for sale. *Check.* Change of will. *Check.* I kept the email subject factual to "Hotmail Natalie" and the tone stripped of emotion, and I ended with: *All future contact is through my lawyer.*

Ten minutes later the phone rang. I let it go to message.

"So you've stooped to the lowest low and locked me out. I told people you wouldn't. I believed in you. Right. You want war? A little visit from the boys perhaps? The KAI? UFF? All it takes is one phone call. I'll gladly go back to Rathcoole and stay with Mum, away from a rich spoiled prat.

"If you touch my stuff, my books and papers—

"Jesus, Cat. Pet, think about it. What are you doing to us?

"You'll never get published without me. Do you hear me, Cat?

"I knew you were crazy. You'll never get over your grief.

"Hoorbeg."

Until finally, his last message: "You are dead to me, Cat."

The following day I went to the RUC Station to file a restraining order. I had my proof—the telephone threats, the times he'd grabbed me. Disobeying the law would ruin his getting back to America. He needed to be clean. He needed to obey.

Theater Natalie. Handpicked by Natalie.

The "other" other woman was becoming my way out.

I stood at the doorway of his study. Signed poetry collections, signed first editions, manila folders with drafts of his poems, manuscripts from the poets he wanted to publish, pocket-sized notebooks.

His belongings were in my hands. I could do what I wanted.

Burn them in the fireplace, sheet by sheet, watch them shrivel and smoke before turning to ash in the grate.

The thought of it warmed.

So this is what power feels like.

A smaller house, a different house. Perhaps a little flat near Sally. She'd told me about a job opening at Oxfam. "You'd be perfect for it, Caitlin," she'd said, eager for me to stay. My interview for the position went well. I knew it had. "Fingers crossed," Sally had said. And then the answer came: "We're sorry, Caitlin. You're perfect for the job, but we need to hire someone from here."

I tried connecting with Tornley. Posted a letter. No reply. What did I have to offer him? People take the side that suits their needs.

But when the sting went away I understood what lay underneath. Tornley had replied by not replying. *Take the goodwill but don't get tied to it and ask for more.* I thought back to the evening he'd invited me to read from the anthology. He knew I belonged behind the podium with the other writers— that I was good enough to belong.

But the girls? I had no choice. He would always be their father.

No final goodbye. No matter. I'd done that before.

She was already in the hospital when I was pulled from university during Christmas exams, the pneumonia pooling her lungs. She didn't know I was there, sitting beside her, as she lay in her morphine-induced gibberish state. The stench of decay permeating the room as her blue eyes rolled back in their sockets.

"Be careful tonight," I'd said to Dad when he backed the Caddy out of the carport. Though I did wave goodbye, I didn't say it.

At least I'd seen the girls one more time, a routine weekend before Andy's departure for America. At the end: *goodbye.* But they couldn't have known.

Dolls for Chel. The piano for Grace. *Tell Me the Colour of Love* for them both.

I sent my commissioned poem to Patrick. I knew Andy wouldn't include it in the art and poetry book, but I wanted him to receive my words. I thought of the last line: *Where does light emerge?*

Three days after Mom died, Dad saw her again. Dream-stunned and disoriented, he'd sat up in his king-size bed and watched a light move towards him from down the dark hallway. Warm rays pulsed through his grieving body. *Russ, that you?* He knew the answer. He wasn't scared. He wanted to touch her, hold her, hear her soft voice, but his body was frozen until she released him, and when he was able to move the light was gone.

Love is all colours wrapped into one. Love is both the prism and the light.

Even Nana was helping me through this. She'd appeared in my dream the moment she was dying. She was the cold eye inside me that knew all along.

Enough!

Yes, Nana. Enough.

Settled in my window seat I looked past the runway towards a strip of grass and saw a slip of motion—a rabbit rummaging the greens.

There was one surviving rabbit on the lawn in Grimsby. Mom brought her upstairs, stunned and safe, set her on her lap on the striped tea towel, and fed her with an eyedropper. I watched the pinched drops fall into her tiny mouth, the tiny ripples along her tiny neck.

I kept Hopper in a cardboard box on the front screened-in porch. I held her in my cupped hands. Her long thin-skinned ears, backlit, veined with red. I could see inside her. Her fur was softer than all my stuffed animals. Tipped on her back I watched her pumping heart. And poops! Out like balls of chocolate, like beads of plasticine.

I didn't want to let go of this gift from the wild, but she was growing and soon she'd outgrow her cardboard box.

But that cat, that neighbouring cat.

Shortly after Mom's hospital visit, her first "woman's operation," we moved to a house beside a water-filled limestone quarry, a mini-lake surrounded by trees, the house of her dreams. Wildlife abounded—fox, osprey, deer—but no cats.

The day was coming. I knew it was coming. *Keep her longer and she'll lose her natural ways.* So I took her out back, near the cluster of evergreen, blue spruce and cedar, and I let her loose on the freshly cut lawn. *She'll remember the smell, the green blades.*

"Go!" I said.

She took her time. Wiggling her whiskers, she sniffed the grass until slowly, gingerly, she hopped away from me.

The plane rose, high above the runway, above the water, beyond the forty greens.

VI

I thought I'd lost it and there it was—the three-heart necklace I'd bought in Larne, tucked in the folds of my mother's green quilt. When I lifted the cord, the hearts—pink, blue, and slate grey—remained on the bed. Was it broken? I yanked at the cord and inspected the knot. *Completely intact.* I picked up the hearts one at a time and inspected the holes for splits. I eyed closely, carefully.

The three hearts were separated, whole, perfect.

Acknowledgements

I am grateful to many people who helped this book come into being, including those who gave feedback during the early stages. Special thanks to Jennifer and Derek Mccullough, Caryl and Richard Williamson, Paul and Pauline Burgess, and John and Cherie Whitaker. I'd also like to thank Kathleen McCracken, Kelli Deeth, Kim Echlin, Jennifer Barclay, Bruce Hunter, Ken Murray, Allyson Latta, Jeanette Lynes, Christine Saratsiotis, Ayesha Chatterjee, Stephenie Gillingham, Kristan Graham-Seymour, and the wonderful Palimpsest team: Aimée Parent Dunn, Ellie Hastings, Theo Hummer, and my laser-eye editor, Ginger Pharand. This book is dedicated to the greatest gift of my life: John Coates.

Notes

"Good fences make good neighbors," Robert Frost, "Mending Wall," *The Poetry of Robert Frost Edited by Edward Connery Lathem,* Holt, Rinehart and Winston, 1969

"Like a long-legged fly upon the stream / her mind moves in silence," W.B. Yeats, "Long-Legged Fly," *Yeats's Poems, Edited and annotated by A. Norman Jeffares* Papermac, Macmillan Publishers Limited, 1989

"What is love? Baby don't hurt me…" Dee Dee Halligan and Junior Torello, "What Is Love?" 1993

"Swear by what the sages spoke / Round the Mareotic Lake," W. B. Yeats, "Under Ben Bulben," *Yeats's Poems, Edited and annotated by A. Norman Jeffares* Papermac, Macmillan Publishers Limited, 1989

"When we did what we did, and the round moon entered and took us in," Catherine Graham, "Between His Finger & His Thumb," *Her Red Hair Rises with the Wings of Insects*, Wolsak and Wynn, 2013

"On limestone quarried near the spot / By his command these words are cut: / Cast a cold eye / On life, on death. / Horseman, pass by!" W. B. Yeats, "Under Ben Bulben," *Yeats's Poems, Edited and annotated by A. Norman Jeffares* Papermac, Macmillan Publishers Limited, 1989

"I close my eyes and picture / the emerald of the sea," Johnny Cash, "Forty Shades of Green," 1959

"A thing of beauty is a joy for ever," John Keats, "Endymion," *The Poetical Works of John Keats,* New York, Thomas Y. Crowell & Company, Publishers, 1895

"With beaded bubbles winking at the brim," John Keats, "Ode to a Nightingale," *The Poetical Works of John Keats,* New York, Thomas Y. Crowell & Company, Publishers, 1895

"Crying cockles and mussels, alive, alive, oh." "Molly Malone," James Yorkston, 1883

"... all perfume yes and his heart was going like mad and yes I said yes I will Yes." *Ulysses*, James Joyce, Shakespeare and Company, 1922

"But I, being poor, have only my dreams; / I have spread my dreams under your feet; /Tread softly because you tread on my dreams." W.B. Yeats. "He Wishes for the Cloths of Heaven." *Yeats's Poems, Edited and annotated by A. Norman Jeffares,* Papermac, Macmillan Publishers Limited, 1989

"Niagarously roaring." Patrick Kavanagh, "Lines Written on a Seat on the Grand Canal, Dublin," *Collected Poems,* Martin Brian & O'Keefe Ltd, 1984

"World is suddener than we fancy it." Louis MacNeice, "Snow," *Collected Poems 1925-1948*, Faber and Faber, 1954

"Turning and turning in the widening gyre / The falcon cannot hear the falconer," W.B. Yeats, "The Second Coming," *Yeats's Poems, Edited and annotated by A. Norman Jeffares* Papermac, Macmillan Publishers Limited, 1989

"Grief is like waiting for fifty giant black kettles to boil." Catherine Graham, "Black Kettles," *Pupa,* Insomniac Press, 2003

"The mass of men lead lives of quiet desperation." Henry David Thoreau, *Walden and Civil Disobedience,* Riverside Editions, 1960

"Take one out for every worry. Let them worry while you sleep. In her dreams the dolls grow angry—*we have worries for you to keep.*" Catherine Graham, "Worry Dolls," *Pupa*, Insomniac Press, 2003

"Where does light emerge?" Catherine Graham, "Visitant," *Pupa,* Insomniac Press, 2003

Catherine Graham is a novelist, poet, and creative writing instructor. Her debut novel, *Quarry*, was a finalist for the Sarton Women's Book Award for Contemporary Fiction and Fred Kerner Book Award and won the Miramichi Reader's "The Very Best!" Book Award and an Independent Publisher Book Awards' gold medal for Fiction. She is the author of seven acclaimed poetry collections, including Æther: *An Out-of-Body Lyric*, a finalist for the Toronto Book Award, *The Celery Forest*, a CBC Best Book of the Year and finalist for the Fred Cogswell Award for Excellence in Poetry, and *Her Red Hair Rises with the Wings of Insects*, a finalist for the Raymond Souster Award and CAA Poetry Award. Her poems have been translated into Greek, Serbo-Croatian, Bangla, Chinese, and Spanish and have appeared internationally. She teaches creative writing at the University of Toronto, where she won an Excellence in Teaching Award. A previous winner of the Toronto International Festival of Authors' Poetry NOW competition, she leads their monthly book club and interviews for By the Lake Book Club. Visit her online at www.catherinegraham.com and @catgrahampoet.